HOOKED ON BOOKS
QUALITY USED BOOKS
ACADEMY & MAIZELAND
COLORADO SPRINGS, CO 80909
(303) 596-1621

Look for upcoming titles in the
Velvet Glove Series

Velvet Glove

10

Jolene Prewit-Parker
Forbidden Dreams

AVON
PUBLISHERS OF BARD, CAMELOT, DISCUS AND FLARE BOOKS

AVON BOOKS
A division of
The Hearst Corporation
1790 Broadway
New York, New York 10019

Copyright © 1984 by Meredith Bernstein & Denise Marcil
Published by arrangement with Velvet Glove, Inc.
Library of Congress Catalog Card Number: 84-90968
ISBN: 0-380-89466-1

First Avon Printing, November 1984

AVON TRADEMARK REG. U.. S. PAT. OFF. AND IN
OTHER COUNTRIES, MARCA REGISTRADA, HECHO EN
U. S. A.

Printed in the U. S. A.

WFH 10 9 8 7 6 5 4 3 2 1

To Bill, my mother and dad,
and my inspirational
muse.

Chapter One

ASHTON PARO warily steered the compact rented car out of one serpentine loop and into the next. West Virginia certainly had its share of hills and sharp turns, but the hairpin curves in western North Carolina would make Mario Andretti shudder, she decided. She kept her eyes riveted to the two narrow lanes ahead. The sedan in front of her was undoubtedly ferrying a load of tourists, for at every bend the driver would slow down and point out a scenic vista and his passengers would lean toward the windows to look. Thirty miles had never seemed to take so long! Already, she had been traveling west on Highway 64 for well over an hour, which was almost as much time as the entire flight from Bluefield down to Asheville had taken. The snail's pace at which she was creeping along confirmed an opinion she had formed long ago: automobiles are a means of convenient transportation, but certainly not a means of pleasure.

Oh, well, might as well enjoy the scenery, too, she decided, rolling down her window. Impatience would not get her to her destination any faster. It was half past eleven now. Perhaps, she thought wryly, if she were lucky she'd make it to Fox Run in time for supper!

Ashton welcomed the fresh air with a smile. How good it felt to have the wind tousling her mane of gypsy ringlets. She took a deep breath and exhaled it slowly. The scent of balsam in the crisp autumn chill was invigorating.

7

Already she was beginning to relax, and the feeling was reflected in the face staring back at her in the rearview mirror. Eyes that only yesterday had showed about as much vigor as melted chocolate drops now danced with new life. A dusty rose blush was returning to her cheeks, and once again her firm, well defined features broadcast a confident, determined air.

For the first time in a long while, Ashton didn't feel as high-strung as a thoroughbred at the starting gate. Returning to the field after a year's stint as chief geologist in charge of mining operations for *Consolidated Minerals* would be just as therapeutic for her as a vacation—maybe even more so! The demands and pressures accompanying her rapid rise up the corporate ladder had begun to take their toll on her a few months earlier. She had realized then that a change of pace was just what she needed to put the gusto back into her work. And what better place to get away from it all than in a town named Fox Run?

How right she had been to take on this gallium project herself instead of assigning it to one of her assistants. The countryside was picture-postcard perfect. A great granite sentinel—Pisgah Mountain, according to the road map— stood guard over the rolling hills and valley. Meadows dotted with haystacks stretched out in the distance. Cows grazed at the front porches of ramshackle farmhouses, and horses ran free in the wind.

A few miles further, the road slowly began to uncoil. A state signpost heralded her entrance into Transylvania County.

Ashton smiled to herself. Being in Transylvania County on Halloween seemed most appropriate.

No sooner had the double yellow line disappeared from the road than a silver pickup came barreling along beside her. She glanced, annoyed, in its direction. Painted on the passenger door was the head of a wolf and the words WOLF LAIR. She looked up at the driver. He answered her scowl with a lopsided grin before accelerating past.

Ashton turned her attention to a whitewashed road sign

coming up on her right. She read the neat, printed letters aloud:

"WELCOME TO FOX RUN, NORTH CAROLINA, LAND OF WATERFALLS AND WHITE SQUIRRELS."

"White squirrels . . . huh . . . white squirrels."

Why an oddity such as a white squirrel should seem so familiar was puzzling. Had she ever seen one, she was certain, she would have remembered such an unusual little creature. It was probably just another tidbit of information she had stored subconsciously, she decided, as she drove into a gas station just beyond the welcome marker.

Ashton pulled up to the self-service island. She was surprised to see that the silver pickup that had zoomed past her minutes earlier was parked in front of the bay.

Inserting the nozzle into the tank, she casually glanced in the direction of the truck. The dark-haired man standing beside it could easily have been cast in a television commercial as a rugged, woodsy type promoting unfiltered cigarettes.

He caught her look and lifted his hand in acknowledgement. "You look familiar," he called out. The lopsided grin was still on his face as he strode toward her.

Ashton found herself taking in every inch of him as he approached. The features of his face were boldly defined and even at a distance were unmistakably sensuous. He possessed the beautifully proportioned physique of an athlete, and he moved with such an easy, self-assured grace that a slight limp in his left leg actually seemed natural.

"At the speed you were traveling, I'm surprised you could see more than a blur," she said lightly, unable to resist.

"You'd be surprised at just what I did see," he returned pleasantly.

A half-hearted grin tugged at her mouth. Apparently, her poison-arrow glare hadn't hit its mark.

Ashton could feel his eyes flicking over every inch of her five-foot five-inch frame. He seemed to be sizing her up, but for what, she wondered. At least he didn't ask if he could give her a hand!

The meter clicked. She topped off the tank to an even amount of fuel, grateful for the opportunity to concentrate on something other than the presence of the man next to her.

He waited until she had returned the nozzle to the pump before he held out his hand. "I'm Cav Cavanaugh."

She looked straight into his eyes. "Ashton Paro." She was aware of holding his hand a moment longer than she would have normally. The reason why was no mystery to her. His eyes did much more than see. They caressed!

"You live around here?" he asked.

The way he casually lounged against the back end of the car made her even more aware of the hips that streamlined into muscular thighs.

Ashton shook her head. "I'm visiting. I'll be here until Thursday," she added, wondering even as she spoke what had possessed her to volunteer that bit of information. It took her only seconds to find the answer to her own question. There was a forceful quality about him that seemed as if it could crumble the most sturdy of feminine defense.

He handed her the gas cap, his fingers brushing hers.

She felt her pulse quicken. Color rushed to her face. Even his touch was virile!

"Thanks," she managed, fumbling the cap into place.

He straightened his stance. "You're welcome."

Her heart pounded against her chest. His very presence commanded attention. Her mind went a total blank, and for what was probably the first time in her life she could think of nothing clever to say.

She flipped the tank cover shut. She didn't want just to say good-bye. She wanted to say something to hold him there, but what? After all, they had only just met. "Well, nice meeting you," she finally said lamely.

He stuffed his hands inside the pockets of his ski vest. She couldn't help but notice the way his broad chest strained against the blue down-filled fabric.

"Nice meeting you, too, but this isn't good-bye, you know."

Her left brow arched high. No, I don't know, she wanted to reply.

Humor flashed in his eyes as he explained. "In a town the size of Fox Run, people are running into each other all the time."

His crooked grin still intact, he strode away, leaving her to wonder if the wink accompanying his wave were deliberate, or if it were some sort of involuntary reflex. One thing was certain, though. That little flick of his eyelid had sure sent her heart into a gallop.

Ashton grabbed her purse from the passenger seat without removing her gaze from his departing figure. The way his legs strained the corduroy jeans would send tingles down any woman's spine. His thighs looked as if they were about to rip right through the material with each long step he took. Maybe his parting prediction would hold true. She wouldn't mind that at all. A man like him could easily make her forget the philosophy she had adopted several years ago, which rated men near the bottom of her list of priorities.

She turned and walked briskly over to the gas station attendant. There was a lot to be said about a life free from the complexities of romantic entanglements, but as Cav Cavanaugh's truck wheeled out of the station, she couldn't remember exactly what.

"Eight dollars of unleaded," she announced to the gray-whiskered man slumped over the counter. He pocketed the money without looking up from his game of solitaire.

Remembering that *Consolidated Minerals* was a stickler for an exact accounting of expense money, she asked for a receipt. He scribbled one out, without taking his eyes off the cards.

"Thanks." She pointed out the window to an ivory-colored squirrel that was trapezing through a tangle of oak branches. "So that's Fox Run's claim to fame?"

The old man's rough veneer cracked and he gave her a

toothless grin. "Folks say them little critters belonged to a road show that passed through here back during the Depression. Somebody left their cages open, and now there's a whole slew of them roaming over—" He stopped in mid-sentence. Watery blue eyes squinted at her with such intensity that she wondered if she had offended him in some way.

"Is something wrong?"

The expression on his leathery face remained unchanged. "Say, you're from around these parts, aren't you?"

She shook her head. "No. I'm from West Virginia. Why do you ask?"

"West Virginny, huh?" He leaned across the counter for a better look. A wad of chewing tobacco rolled from one side of his mouth to the other and back again. "You know, you look just like a gal that used to live here. I could have sworn . . . naw, never mind. Can't be."

"Can't be what?" she asked, curious for him to explain his remark.

His shoulders sagged even more as he backed away. "Nothing. Just can't be. That's all."

Ashton could feel his beady eyes drilling holes in her even after she was seated inside the automobile. She looked back in the rearview mirror as she pulled away from the pump. The old man was standing in the doorway, his mouth hanging open. The look of bewilderment plastered across his face made Ashton wonder if a visitor to Fox Run were as strange an occurrence as a white squirrel would have been back home.

The outskirts of Fox Run lay just beyond a row of rain-gullied fields where stray stalks of corn stood interspersed among the dried and withered stubble. A knowing smile parted Asthon's lips ever so slightly as she entered what there was of the town's business district. The town was just as sedate as she had envisioned upon first hearing its name. And it was the promise of such a sedate setting that had drawn her to Fox Run in the first place. Progress had yet to disturb the napping community. Quaint specialty shops named for the owners and the services they rendered stood in place of chain stores and fast-food restaurants. Had it not been for a few late-model automobiles scattered along Main Street, Ashton could have been convinced that she had been transported back into another era.

She drove right to her first stop. The Transylvania County Courthouse was located where she had expected to find it, centered on the town square among a grove of maples that had already lost most of their regalia of fall colors.

Ashton zipped the rental car into a parking space, then hopped out of the car. She belted her leather coat tightly around her camel-hair dress and tucked her purse under her arm. A pair of signal cannons in front of the courthouse attracted her interest, and she paused at the entranceway to admire them. Once inside the antebellum building, she skimmed the row of office doors for one marked *Register of Deeds.*

A girl whose face was all but hidden by a Farrah Fawcett hairdo glanced over the top of her movie magazine when Ashton walked into the office. "We're closed until one-thirty."

Ashton checked her watch. She hoped the registrar wasn't in the habit of extending his lunch hour. "I'll wait."

"Suit yourself."

Ashton sat down and thumbed through a coverless magazine.

The door to the office opened again a short while later. Ashton glanced up. From the corner of her eye she caught sight of a pair of gray corduroy legs that looked very familiar.

"Hi, Beth Ann. Is Fred around?"

Even had she not turned around and seen Cav standing there, Ashton could not have mistaken that voice.

"Gee, Cav, I'm real sorry, but he isn't back from lunch." The secretary shook her hair out of her eyes. "I could call him down at the cafe if you'd like."

Ashton cut her eyes to the counter. She had been waiting nearly a half hour, and that courtesy hadn't been extended to her!

"Don't bother him." Cav glanced at the couch. "I'll wait." He walked away from the counter. His smile spread wider with each step he took. "I'll bet you think I'm following you."

Ashton grinned. "You already prepared me for that. Remember?"

"So I did." He sat down beside her. "Maybe we should exchange itineraries and then carpool the rest of the day."

"That's a thought." She noticed his eyes were the same deep brown as her own.

"Are you waiting on Fred?"

Ashton sensed that his friendliness was sincere and not just a front to mask a calculated come-on. "I'm waiting on whoever can supply me with some maps."

"Maps of what?"

"Transylvania County." When he did not question her answer, Ashton added a rehearsed explanation. "I understand this area is a hiker's paradise. As long as I'm in Fox Run, I might do some exploring."

"I learned how to use a compass and read maps in Boy Scouts," he announced matter-of-factly.

"We were taught more than cookie baking in Girl Scouts," she could not resist declaring.

"What do you think of Fox Run so far?" Cav asked.

"I grew up in a town in West Virginia that's about the same size as this, so I feel pretty much at home." Usually she wasn't one for small talk, but now she found herself welcoming the chance to chat for a while. She supposed it was the company that was making the difference.

"What town was that?"

"Bluefield."

"That's a mining town, isn't it?"

She nodded.

"Are you involved in mining?"

"Indirectly."

Ashton knew she was being evasive. She told herself that she didn't have any choice in the matter. Her boss had given her explicit instructions to remain close-mouthed about her reasons for being in Fox Run. Property owners in rural areas were notorious for jacking up prices when an outsider showed an interest in purchasing land. Besides, she knew from previous dealings that if word got out why she was there, a few of *Consolidated*'s competitors were not above sabotaging her efforts in Fox Run.

The relief Ashton felt when Cav did not press the issue turned to disappointment when he withdrew a folded newspaper from his hip pocket and turned his attention to it with a mumbled, "I see." She returned to her own reading knowing that she had only herself to blame for ending the conversation on such an abrupt note.

Concentrating on the article proved to be an exercise in futility. The name Cav Cavanaugh sounded in her ears like a broken record. There was something very familiar about that name, but she just couldn't put her finger on what made her think so.

Curiosity finally got the best of her, and she slanted the magazine so that she could view him from a better angle without being too conspicuous. She knew she had heard that name before, but where?

Ashton appraised her subject critically. The most distinctive feature of his profile, she decided, was that it was clean-cut. His hair was the same color as his eyes, and it fell to a conservative length above his collar. He was neither a small man nor a large one, but the hardness of his body kept him from being described as merely average. His features lacked the flawless good looks that fashion magazines exploited, yet there was something about him that would make him stand out in any crowd. He was handsome enough, but it was his earthiness that gave him character.

Confident that Cav was too involved in the cover story of the *Transylvania Times* to detect her, Ashton ventured out from behind her camouflage. She remembered to turn a page to keep up appearance. Whoever said that man cannot be judged by his clothes hadn't used Cav as an example! While his outfit was sensible for the mountain cold, it could not be considered ordinary. The flannel and corduroy hugged him like they had been tailor-made to a perfect fit. She would wager that he didn't own a single pullover with an alligator on it—and she was confident that the reason was not that he couldn't afford them. The fine quality of his boots told her otherwise. She suspected that, like his clothes, Cav Cavanaugh was basically very unpretentious.

Ashton sensed a few moments later that Cav's head was about to turn, but she couldn't prepare herself in time.

He flashed her a lopsided grin that could have charmed a cobra.

She felt her face reflect the red plaid of his shirt. "The only excuse I have for my rudeness is that I was trying to figure out why your name should ring a bell with me."

Cav chuckled but said nothing.

"Don't I at least get a hint?"

The sun freckles dusted across his nose came alive. "Flipper."

She repeated the clue. "As in porpoise?"

"As in synonym for."

Ashton snapped her fingers. "Of course. You're the kicker for the *Dolphins.*"

Cav was quick to correct her. "Was. Past tense. I retired after the eighty season."

He stretched his arm out over the top of the couch and rested it a few inches away from her shoulders, and Ashton felt like Mexican jumping beans were turning cartwheels in her stomach.

"Nineteen-eighty . . . that was the year the Jets zapped Miami's chances for going to the playoffs. Right?" she asked.

"So the lady's an avid football fan with a great memory!"

"Yes to the first part, but no to the second. I can't even remember what I had for dinner last night." She shifted a bit in her seat. "To be honest with you, the reason I remember that particular game so well is because I was there."

He looked impressed.

"You see, my dad flew a charter down to Miami for the game, and he invited me along to keep him company."

"A real father-daughter outing," he said with a smile.

"Something like that."

He leaned closer. "Tell me the truth. Who were you rooting for?"

"I plead the fifth."

"You sure know how to shatter a guy's ego."

Ashton chuckled. She had been told that before, but the circumstances hadn't been nearly as friendly. "If it makes you feel any better, those three-pointers you kicked from mid-field were very impressive."

"But you weren't impressed enough to cheer for me, were you?" he teased.

"Sorry, but had I made the least bit of a fuss, I would have had to find other transportation home." Her brows knitted together for a second. There was something else about Miami's kicker that she remembered, something other than his skill. The entire defensive line of the *Jets* had converged on him before he had had a chance to try to put the game into overtime. Hadn't he limped off the field to a standing ovation? She had a feeling Miami had lost much more than a shot at the Super Bowl that day. It had cost them the league's best kicker!

Cav read her thoughts. "That was the last game I played in."

Ashton could detect no bitterness or regret in his tone. His remark was purely a statement of fact. "The transition from player to spectator must have been difficult," she said, breaking the silence.

Legs that were still as firm and as solid as any athlete's stretched out in front of him. "It was, but I was luckier than most."

"How so?"

"I was able to accept it."

Experience had taught Ashton to reserve judgment on a person until she knew more about him, but her feminine intuition told her that she knew enough about Cav Cavanaugh to like him very much. Perhaps too much.

Cav stood up.

There was no mistaking the reason for the gnawing at her insides. Cav was the first male who had piqued her feminine interest in a long time. And, he had done it without even trying! Most of her male colleagues viewed her as a rival. Men in unrelated fields seemed just as threatened by her. Cav appeared to be a notch or two above all that! She was sorry at the thought that she probably wouldn't have the chance to get to know him better.

"You know, Ashton Paro, you strike me as a very independent woman." A mischievous gleam played in his eyes. "I bet if I asked you to lunch, you would insist on going dutch."

Her eyes reflected the sparkle of his. "If that's an invitation, I accept."

Chapter Two

ASHTON knew the minute she stepped inside Varner's that she had instantly become the topic of lunchtime conversation. The sound of the bell above the door had caused heads to turn in idle curiosity, but then stools began to swivel and sandwiches to halt in mid-air. Facial expressions perked up, and the casual chatter dwindled to a low hum.

Aware that every eye in the restaurant was on her, Ashton threaded her way through the maze of tables. It seemed to her that the harder she tried to silence the clicking of her heels across the checkerboard tiles, the louder it became.

Her eyes straight ahead, she aimed for the rear of the grill and retreated inside a booth. "Whatever happened to down-home hospitality?" she mumbled to Cav as he slid in, not across from her, but beside her. She didn't know whether she should be flattered or insulted by the rude stares.

Cav laughed. "Fox Run doesn't get many visitors."

"I can certainly see why," she returned, frowning.

Cav's hand swallowed hers. "Hey, don't take it personally. It's just the way things are around here."

Ashton nodded. She understood perfectly well what he meant by that remark. Her work had taken her to many mountain communities, most of them in Appalachia, and the reception she was given was almost always the same.

"Unless you were born here, you don't ever really belong," she said, verbalizing her thoughts.

"Exactly," he agreed with a grin. "Take me, for instance. I've lived here for three years, and I still have the feeling these folks only tolerate me." He squeezed her hand reassuringly. "Don't worry about them, though. I'm not a bad welcoming committee on my own."

Her entire arm felt empty when he released those few fingers. The odd sensations aroused by his touch made her decide to devote her attention to the person sitting with her inside the booth, and to heck with those on the outside!

"Hey, I thought you said you were going to feed me," she reminded him, elbowing his arm. "I'm starved."

Chuckling, Cav motioned to a slim, middle-aged woman who was standing behind the counter.

The woman gave him a tired wave and took a couple of plastic menus from the bar. Chatting with a few of the regulars, she padded towards the rear booth. Her fuchsia colored lips froze in place when she was several tables away. Her cheeks paled beneath the vibrant blush of her rouge, and her dark eyes opened wide. She covered the last few yards slowly, cautiously, and looking as though she were certain something dreadful was about to jump out and grab her at any minute.

After jotting down their order for two burger baskets and peanut-butter shakes, she tucked her pen into the red hair piled on top of her head. "Sorry I was gawking at you a minute ago, hon," she told Ashton, the color returning to her face. "Seeing you here caught me a little off guard. You're the spitting image of a gal that used to live in town," she explained, in answer to Ashton's look of confusion.

"How odd! The man at the gas station told me the same thing," Ashton remarked thoughtfully. "Isn't that funny?"

The waitress's cheeks hollowed. "Pop? What else did he say?" Wrinkles popped out all over her face.

"Nothing. Just that I looked like someone who used to

live in Fox Run." Her brow knitted. "Why? Should he have said something else?"

The woman looked relieved. "Oh, no, not at all," she replied quickly. She stuffed her pad into the frilled pocket of her pink apron. "Pop has a tendency to flirt with pretty young customers. Seeing as how you're new in town, I just didn't want you to get the wrong impression. That's all."

Ashton chuckled to herself. "No chance of that." The impression he had given her, she remembered, was that she couldn't get out of the station fast enough to suit him. "Do you know this woman I'm supposed to resemble?" she asked Cav.

He thought for a minute, then shook his head. "No, can't say as I do."

Ashton turned her attention to the waitress. "I wish I could meet her. You and Pop have certainly aroused my curiosity." Not only that, she decided silently, but the idea that she should resemble someone so closely was most interesting.

"Myra!" blared a brash voice from the front of the grill. "Are you going to stand there yakking all day or are you going to fix my lunch?"

Myra snapped to attention. "Be right with you, Mr. Breyer." Looking like a whipped puppy, she shuffled away from the booth.

Ashton wrinkled her nose in distaste. "What a pleasant-sounding fellow! Who is he?"

"Hampton Breyer. The third, I think," answered Cav with a trace of sarcasm. "When he talks, people listen."

"Huh. Just what every town needs—it's own E.F. Hutton."

Myra returned a few minutes later and set their shakes down in front of them without a mumble.

Ashton wanted to cheer her up with a compliment or a kind word but then decided against embarrassing the poor woman any more than she already was. Instead, she thanked her quietly.

"What makes Hampton Breyer the third so powerful?"

She speared her straw into the thick foam. "Does he own the town?"

Cav shook his head. "Worse than that. He's the only lawyer in the whole county."

Ashton nodded understandingly. "So it's not who you know here, but what you know about them."

"You got it!"

She repeated the lawyer's name to herself, then said it aloud a moment later.

Cav answered the unspoken question she had already posed to herself. "It probably sounds familiar because it's plastered across nearly every signpost and billboard from here to Asheville. He's a candidate for State Senate."

She stirred her shake thoughtfully. "That must be it." Curious for a better look, she peered over the top of the booth. Her inquisitive glance was met with razor-sharp eyes that sliced right through her. She slid back down in her seat. No one had to tell her who he was! That face had a definite air of superiority.

"Mr. Breyer sure could use a few pointers from *How To Win Friends and Influence People,*" she said, sipping her drink. "Is he always so charming?"

Cav laughed. "Believe it or not, when he's out politicking he draws more crowds than a tent revival."

Ashton simply could not accept Cav's analogy, especially when she saw the way Myra approached their table a short while later. The poor woman's eyes scarcely left her feet when she walked past Breyer.

"Are you alright?" asked Ashton gently.

Myra nodded, put down their lunch, and backed away, all in the same motion. Ashton watched her, frowning.

Cav tapped her shoulder and pointed to the burger basket in front of her. "I thought you were starved."

"I am!" she exclaimed, startled from her thoughts. She reached for her hamburger. Trying to figure out why the waitress had shied was pointless, anyway. Chances were, Myra had to deal with customers even more obnoxious than Breyer, she told herself.

Ashton eyed her hamburger after taking the first bite. "I can just feel those calories. All two thousand of them."

"I don't know why you should be worried," said Cav between bites. "You look just fine to me."

She smiled to herself. The next time she worried about that extra inch on her hips, she'd remember that. She glanced at her companion while she chewed. He looked even more appetizing. She stiffled a giggle. And not nearly as fattening!

"One more french fry and I'll turn into a giant spud," she laughed, leaning back from the table a while later. Her head resting against the back of the booth, she watched as he finished his meal. "Tell me, how did a cracker boy like you end up in the mountains?"

He brushed his napkin over his mouth. "After thirty-two years in Florida, ten of them spent in Miami, I was ready for a change of scenery."

"But why Fox Run?"

"There's a lot of potential in this area for land development," he answered thoughtfully.

She remembered the wolf's head and the lettering on his pickup. "Is that what you're involved in here? Land development?"

"Indirectly."

Ashton grinned. His answer struck home. "Touché, Mr. Cavanaugh. I deserved that."

His arms folded across his chest. "I couldn't agree with you more."

She waited, but he said nothing. "Well?"

"What we have here is a standoff." He leaned closer. His breath was warm against her cheek. His scent was manly and intoxicating. "I asked you first. Remember?"

She nodded. Cav had succeeded in intriguing her. Few men ever did that! "You win," she acquiesced. "I'm a geologist."

His expression remained unchanged. His quiet acceptance surprised her. That declaration had caused more than one sexist dig to be directed at her.

"Did your work bring you to western North Carolina?" he asked finally.

She had anticipated his next question and had already decided how it should be answered. It didn't take someone with ESP to sense that Cav was a man who could be trusted.

Once again, she nodded. "Satellite mappings of this area have reported deposits of a metal called gallium. I'm here to determine if the concentration warrants a full-scale investigation."

"Ah, so that's the reason for the secrecy." He chuckled to himself. "All that time I thought you were playing hard to get."

"Disappointed?"

"Not at all. I'm relieved." His eyes locked onto hers briefly. "Tell me, is this gallium a metal common in the United States?"

Ashton was slow in answering. His gaze had been so penetrating. Was she reading more into it than was actually there? It took her a few seconds to collect her thoughts. "No, gallium is not common in this country. Substantial deposits have been found only in the southwest." She found herself searching his eyes for the spark she had just seen. Concentrating on her subject became difficult. Her eyes were conscious of his. Her answer was directed at his chin. "The demand in the United States is still high, but the production and supply are both very low. Most of the gallium we use is imported from Europe."

"That must be expensive."

"Exactly," she nodded. "That's why *Consolidated* is so excited at the prospect of another source in the States."

"And obviously why they're so anxious for you to keep a low profile." His arms folded beside hers. "How is it used?"

His interest was sincere, of that she was certain. His questions were intelligent ones, which showed he considered her an authority and respected her knowledge.

"Until last year, its major use had been in high-tech electronics," she explained. "More recently, however, medical researchers have discovered that a form of gallium will be absorbed by any cancerous part of a bone."

Cav was quick to catch on. "Thus enabling doctors to detect bone cancer in its early stages. . . . Interesting," he nodded thoughtfully. "Tell me, will your study encompass the—"

Ashton lifted her hand in protest. "Whoa! No fair. You have yet to tell me what you've been doing in Fox Run for the last three years. That was part of the bargain, too. Remember?"

"Alright. What would you like to know?" Smiling broadly, he scooted even closer.

The warm, wonderful pressure against her leg snatched her breath away for one quick instant. The heat of his thigh penetrated layers of corduroy, wool, and silk. Moisture beaded against her pantyhose. A special understanding was suddenly flowing freely between them; she sensed that he was as conscious of it as she. It took but a moment for her to regain her composure. "Well, for starters, what is *Wolf Lair?*"

"It's a ski resort. Or, rather, it will be soon." He stretched his arm across the back of the booth. "We open for business Thanksgiving Day."

Her shoulders conformed to the masculine outline with hardly any effort at all. "That certainly sounds exciting. Why did you decide to locate here?"

"I used to come up to a summer camp nearby. I made up my mind then that when I grew up, I'd live here." He chuckled lightly. "It took me a few years, but I finally got around to moving up from the flatlands."

His arm casually molded around her shoulders. Her stomach felt like a hundred butterflies had just been set free inside it. She was as queasy as a co-ed sitting at the soda shop with the big man on campus. She couldn't remember the last time she had experienced such a rush when a man put his arm around her. Trying to show no change of facial expression, she urged him to continue.

"A group of heirs from a very wealthy family had just

put six hundred acres of choice mountain property on the market," he continued. "The minute I saw it, I knew that was the place I wanted to live. I bought the land, fixed up their old hunting cabin and moved into it, and began work on phase one of the *Wolf Lair* project."

"Phase one? You mean there's more than the ski resort?" She felt herself leaning more into his hold and growing more comfortable with each passing second. She couldn't recall the last time she had felt so much at ease with a man. Come to think of it, she couldn't remember the last time a man had appeared so at ease with her!

"There will be." He answered her question with a decisiveness that made her sit up and take notice. "By summer, the first group of condominiums will be ready for occupancy, and land for private building sites will be auctioned off to buyers. Plus, a golf course, three tennis courts, and a stable will be added to the already existing recreational facilities." He stopped and flashed her a big, loppy grin. "Sorry, I sound like a PR man."

"Don't apologize! You should be enthusiastic. And proud! You are undertaking a first-class project!" she remarked admiringly.

"Fortunately for me, I have a great crew and a foreman who's the best in the business. Without them, *Wolf Lair* would exist only on my planning board," he said modestly.

He gave credit where credit was due. She liked that in a man. That was one more trait to add to the list of his virtues that had begun forming in her mind back at the courthouse.

"I'd like to show you the development some time." His fingers outlined the cuff of her sweater-dress. "That is, if you're not too tied up while you're here."

"I'll look forward to it!" she answered quickly. Even if she had little time to spare, she was certain he was worth rearranging her schedule for.

"You'll love Wolf Mountain," he continued. "It's like no other place in the world. It's a great place for hiking, horseback riding, camping—you name it."

She hoped her luck would hold out. "Is it near Bear Wallow Mountain?"

"They're side by side. Why?" He didn't give her a chance to answer. "Don't tell me that's where the gallium is."

She knew immediately that she had struck a raw nerve. "Not the mountain as a whole, mind you. Just the southwestern slope."

His sigh was definitely one of relief. "You had me worried there for a minute."

"I don't understand."

His hand took back her wrist. "I have been trying to buy some of the Bear Wallow property that adjoins mine. So far, the owner has been more than reasonable in our dealings. All that's left to do before the papers are signed is have the land surveyed." He took a deep breath. "However, if he thought a mining company was interested, he might not be so willing to sell at the price we've already agreed on."

Ashton shook her head. "No need to worry about that. The concentration of gallium is confined to that one particular area. *Consolidated* has no interest in any other section, I assure you." She was just as relieved as he—but for entirely different reasons. "Since you know the owner, maybe you could prepare me for what to expect from him. Would he be difficult to deal with?"

Cav's eyes drifted up front. "You'll have to be the judge of that."

Why Hampton Breyer's name had sounded so familiar finally dawned on her. She hadn't noticed it on the billboards, she remembered, feeling for the gold chain around her neck. No, of course not. The name had been listed on the spec sheet for the gallium project. "I think I'll wait until *Consolidated* gives the go ahead before introducing myself," she said as she slid the clasp around to the back of her neck.

"Your secret is safe with me—for the time being," he said with a wink.

"What's that supposed to mean?"

"My silence is not without a price." His eyes danced with merriment. "Either have dinner with me tonight, or be prepared for a full page ad in the *Times* announcing the real reason you've come to Fox Run."

"You don't have to resort to extortion." As a matter of fact, I can't think of anything I'd rather do, she added silently.

His eyes locked with hers. "I thought you'd see things my way."

Little by little, Ashton found all else but his nearness became unimportant. For the time being, nothing else mattered. The booth was their own little fort protecting them from the stares and whispers outside. His breath was warm and inviting, a sultry breeze fanning her cheeks.

Her face lifted in compliance. Lids closed with a sigh.

His kiss was feather light. It was hardly more than a whisper against her lips, but its impact sang through her veins and left her burning with desire for another.

Her lips lifted in a smile. She opened her eyes, and their gazes held in a starry-eyed exchange. Now, she truly knew what it meant to be swept off her feet!

Myra came to collect the money for their lunch.

Ashton pried her eyes from his with a giggle.

"Please note that I made no attempt to reach for my purse," she told Cav afterward.

"Just make sure you bring plenty of money tonight," he said teasingly.

Smiling comfortably, she shook her head. "No way, bucko. He who asks, picks up the check." She caught a glimpse of gray pinstripes headed their way. "Looks like Fox Run's favorite son is coming to visit," she mumbled. She pulled her gaze away from Cav and directed it at Hampton Breyer as he approached.

Tiny furrows etched a permanent scowl on Breyer's mouth. His short cropped hair had as much black as gray, but his stern air made him seem even older. It was easy to imagine him on the Senate floor, addressing his colleagues.

After a brief exchange of pleasantries, he sat down without waiting for an invitation.

Ashton was certain there were very few people in town who would dare to oppose him. He struck her as being hard as nails. She'd sure have her work cut out if *Consolidated* were to decide to negotiate for exploration rights to his property! Just the way his eyes put her under surveillance made her feel as though she were a suspect for some horrible crime.

"So where are you from, Miss Paro?" inquired Breyer pleasantly enough after the introductions had been made.

"West Virginia," she answered in her most businesslike tone.

He flipped the ashes from his cigarette into the aluminum tray without taking his eyes from her for an instant. "Tell me, what are you doing up in our neck of the woods?"

"Just visiting." She purposefully held his stare. He struck her as the sort of man who made it his civic responsibility to interview any and all outsiders.

"Plan on staying long?"

"I haven't decided." She pitied the witnesses he interrogated in court. He could make the victim feel guilty!

Breyer took another cigarette from his pocket. His stare fell on her throat. "What a lovely necklace. A family heirloom?"

Ashton reached for the gold rosebud in a way that had become a habit over the years. "It belonged to my mother."

Breyer took a long drag on his cigarette. "It's very pretty."

"Thank you." When his next question was directed at Cav, she decided that she had passed the visitors' test. She heard the word "business" and decided to make a graceful exit while she still had a chance.

"If you'll excuse me, gentlemen, I have some errands to attend." Her smile was as short as her answers had been. "Mr. Breyer, nice meeting you."

Cav helped her into her coat. "I'll pick you up at the inn at six if that's alright."

"That's fine. See you then." She tucked her purse under her arm, and, after a perfunctory nod, walked away.

Myra was standing behind the cash register. Ashton started to speak, but the waitress motioned for quiet. The woman's eyes darted to the rear of the grill, then back up front again. When Myra finally spoke, her words were barely audible. "Stay away from Hamp Breyer."

Ashton was sure she had misunderstood her. She took a step closer. "What did you say?"

Myra said nothing. She looked toward the back once more, then retreated into the kitchen.

Chapter Three

Ashton drove several blocks past the street she was looking for before she realized that she had missed her turn. Her mind was back at Varner's and had been ever since she had left there two hours ago. At the courthouse after lunch, her concentration had been divided between the survey maps and Myra's odd remark. So far, the only conclusion she could come to was that it made absolutely no sense at all. Granted, Breyer was not Mister Personality Plus, but he hardly seemed that threatening.

She circled the next block and crossed over onto Park Place. She had called the Red Fox Inn earlier for directions, and the instructions she had been given over the phone led her right to a red shuttered house that had a small painted fox on the mailbox.

A calico cat met her at the door and sashayed in and out between her legs until he tired of his game and settled back down on the rug with a lion's yawn.

"Be right down," called out a cheerful voice from above.

Ashton deposited her bags at the stairs and waited. The elderly proprietress who descended the stairs was the perfect picture of a Southern lady. Small in stature, she carried herself erect and proud. She glided down the stairs with grace, her eyes on Ashton and her fingers just skimming the bannister.

Her smile faded a few steps from the bottom. Rosy

cheeks suddenly lost their blush. She stopped and groped for the railing.

Ashton ran up the stairs. "Are you alright?" she asked, taking hold of her arm.

The old woman seemed lost in a daze. "Ashley?"

"Ashton. Ashton Paro. Remember, I called you this morning about a room?" She led her the rest of the way down. "You are Mrs. Sievers, aren't you?"

The woman's color was returning. "No need for formalities around here, dear. Please call me Molly." She pointed the way into the sitting room. "Sorry to give you such a fright, dear," she said, easing down into her rocker. "Must be my low blood pressure acting up again. Doc Warren warned me old age was going to catch up with me sooner or later." Her face brightened. "He thinks I ought to stay home and knit. Can you imagine such a thing?"

Ashton was still concerned. The inn's proprietress still looked a little peaked. "Perhaps I should call him for you."

Molly shook her finger. "Shame on you for even thinking about snitching on me."

"Are you sure you're alright?" asked Ashton, still not convinced.

Molly waved aside her concern. "Don't worry about me. There's nothing wrong that a cup of ginseng tea won't cure." She gave Ashton a gentle shove. "Go sit down. It makes me dizzy having to look up at you."

Ashton found that in no time at all she felt right at home in the sitting room. The burgundy velvet covering the old-fashioned settees and lounges gave the room a warm coziness that modern-day living rooms lacked. Like its owner, the room had aged with dignity.

"Living in a house like this must be every antiquarian's dream," she remarked, surveying the furnishings with an appreciative eye.

Molly beamed. "I'm so glad you like it. Most young people these days don't appreciate remnants from another generation, be it people or furniture. Anything old commands very little respect." She looked very prim and proper with her hands folded in her lap and her back erect. "Tell me, dear, is this your first visit to Fox Run?"

Ashton took an immediate liking to the proprietress. "Yes, it is."

"Will you be staying long?"

"Three or four days at the most," she answered.

Molly suddenly rose from her rocker with the spryness of a woman half her age. "Gracious me! Where are my manners? I haven't even offered you a cup of tea."

"No need to trouble yourself, really," said Ashton.

"Nonsense." Assuring her guest that not every day did she have a chance to take out her good silver, Molly left the room with far more energy than she had entered it.

Her hands locked behind her back, Ashton strolled around the room admiring the memorabilia that had obviously been collected over several lifetimes. Displayed on a credenza in the corner of the parlor was a collection of music boxes. She fell in love with a procelain one that was crowned with a carousel of brightly ribboned ponies.

"What do you think of my collection of pretties?" asked Molly as she reentered the room carrying a silver tray that was almost as big as she.

Ashton could not take her eyes from the music box with the ponies. "They're beautiful!"

Molly sat down and poured their tea. "Please, feel free to wind one up. They do more than collect dust, you know." Ashton carefully lifted the carousel from its place. Her fingers caressed each of the three ponies. "This one's my favorite," she told Molly. She turned the key slowly. Soft strains of Gershwin's *Rhapsody in Blue* filled the room. She hummed along with it, waiting for the tune to end before she spoke. "I played that at my first piano recital," she told Molly as she returned the box to its place.

Molly handed her a dainty tea cup. "Cream?"

"No, thank you."

"Sugar?"

Ashton nodded. "Yes, please."

Molly dropped a cube into the cup, her hand quivering

slightly. She looked up and grinned. "Now you don't go telling Doc Warren that I've got the shakes."

"I won't," Ashton promised.

The old woman settled back against her cushion. "So tell me, my dear, where are you from?"

"Bluefield, West Virginia," she answered, blowing on her tea.

Molly called for her cat. He bounded across the room and into her lap, where he curled up comfortably. "And your folks?"

"They live there as well," she replied. "My dad's retired Navy and my mom's Dean of Women at a small university nearby."

Molly took a long sip. "How about you? Any children?"

Ashton shook her head. "I'm not married."

The old lady stared at her over the rim of her cup. "Any prospects?" she asked, not batting an eye.

Ashton chuckled. Had it been anyone else asking such questions, she would have been annoyed, but she doubted whether anyone could even bring themselves to utter a cross word to someone like Mrs. Sievers, who had the look of a kindly, concerned grandmother down pat. "I'm very choosy," she finally said, laughing.

Molly patted her hand. "So was I. Now, look at me. All I have to keep me warm is old fleabag here. 'Course he's not near as much trouble as a man would be." She eyed Ashton thoughtfully. "I reckon you'd be a career woman."

She nodded. "I'm a geologist."

"I figured you were a professional woman," said Molly with an approving smile. "You have that look about you."

"Oh? What look is that?"

Molly leaned closer. "One that says 'Come hell or high water, I'm going to succeed!' " She smoothed her soft, silvery hair back from her face. "I was a career woman myself."

Ashton glanced at the still lifes and landscapes decorating the walls. "I thought it was too much of a coincidence for your favorite artist to have the same initials as you!"

The years fell away from the old woman's face. She spoke with obvious pride. "Why, I sold to galleries all along the Eastern seaboard. Even went to New York once for a private showing. That was really something risqué for a woman to do back then." Pale gray eyes twinkled blue. "You should have seen the faces of those Yankee stuffed-shirts when M.M. Siever turned out to be a woman."

"You should be drafted for the E.R.A. movement," Ashton chuckled.

Molly waved aside the remark. "What? And have to settle for equality? Heavens, no. I prefer things just the way they are."

The clock on the mantle chimed four times.

"Goodness, me, I had no idea it was getting so late," said Molly, assembling the cups and saucers back on the tray. "Here I've been carrying on like a magpie. You must be worn out from your trip."

"Not at all," Ashton assured her, unable to resist the urge to give Molly's hand a squeeze. "I quite enjoyed our little chat."

"Did you?" Her face lit up. "So did I!" She watched as Ashton stood. "You know, you're a sweet thing. Pretty as a picture, too, and every bit as nice as I knew you'd be."

"As you knew I'd be?"

"Why—yes. I can tell a lot about someone just by her voice. When I spoke with you on the phone, I knew right then that you would be a fine person." She shooed her cat off her lap, then rose quickly. "Come along now, I'll show you to your room. After you've had a nap, I'll fix you some fried chicken for supper, and then later if you're not too tired, we might even play a few hands of rummy," she said, taking her guest by the hand and leading her to a room opposite the stairs.

Ashton felt a little guilty at having to disappoint her. She had obviously been looking forward to the company. Most likely, any visitors who did come to this part of the state by-passed Fox Run in favor of the more popular tourist haunts in Asheville or Hendersonville. Still, she did have her own plans for the evening, she reminded herself.

"Cav Cavanaugh is as fine as they come," remarked Molly after hearing of Ashton's engagement. "You just ask him who makes the best pear cobbler he's ever eaten." She opened the door to the guest room and showed her inside. "I hope it suits you. If not, there are six more you can choose from. I think this one's the nicest, though," she said, proudly motioning to the small brass bed with a yellow and white gingham canopy and spread. "Remember, now, if there's anything you need, don't be shy about asking for it."

"There is something you might be able to help me with," Ashton said after dragging her bags inside.

"Yes?"

She hesitated, not quite sure how to put into words what she wanted to know. "Do I look like anyone you know?" she asked finally.

"What on earth are you talking about?"

She laughed. It sounded pretty silly, even to her. "Well," she began slowly, "Pop down at the gas station mistook me for someone else, then Myra from Varner's told me that I was the spitting image of a girl she used to know."

Molly's hand rested against her cheek. "Hmm. That is odd."

"There's more." She took a deep breath. What she was about to say sounded even stranger. "When I left Varner's, Myra warned me to stay away from Hamp Breyer."

"Hamp Breyer?" Mollie asked, frowning.

She nodded. "He came back to our booth to see Cav, so when they started discussing business, I left."

"Goodness, you've certainly had a busy day getting acquainted with everyone, haven't you?" Molly said. "I don't know what to make of Myra's warning. I hear tell Hamp's quite a lady's man, though, but I can't imagine him setting his sights on you with Cav sitting right there." She paused to think, then shook her head. "I wouldn't pay any mind to Myra. She can be a mite peculiar at times."

"Then I don't resemble anyone you know or have known?"

Molly's finger tapped against the door jamb. "I don't think so. Then again, my memory's not as good as it used to be. I'll think about it, and if anyone comes to mind, I'll be sure to let you know." Molly scooped up her cat. "Come along, Sebastian, we've bothered our company long enough. Remember, dear, if you need anything, just give a holler."

Ashton took one look at her luggage and decided to save the unpacking for tomorrow. A quick stroll around the neighborhood would be just the thing to refresh and relax her before her date with Cav. She quickly changed into a pair of faded jeans and a fisherman's sweater that was several sizes too large, then traded her heels for a pair of English riding boots that had caught the worst of more than one pair of venemous fangs down through the years.

Every breath inhaled outside invigorated her. The cold air was crisp and clean, a revitalizing elixir for the body and soul. She could feel her energy level rising immediately.

She walked past a group of ghosts and goblins and flashed an encouraging smile to the frazzled-looking moms who were shepherding the youngsters from house to house.

A haystack of raked leaves on the next corner proved too inviting to resist. Taking a running start, she leaped feet first right into the center.

A playground across the street caught her eye. Brushing the leaves from her legs, she ran over to it. The gate was unlatched, so she ventured inside.

The park was deserted except for her. Her body temperature suddenly dropped a few degrees right on the spot. Her arms hugging at her waist, she moved past the swings and the monkey bars and made her way to the merry-go-round in the center. Goose bumps the size of eggs prickled her flesh when she sat down on the carousel. Without warning, she was overcome with an eerie feeling of déjà vu, as if she had been there before, as if once before she had sat spinning round and round on the merry-go-round with her hair streaming out behind her.

Shivering, she drew her sweater even tighter. Her scientific nature and her analytical mind could offer no explanation for the way she was feeling.

She walked slowly around the carousel. Perhaps her subconscious was finally allowing her a peek at her early years as a child. Closing her eyes, she tried her best to call back the image that had been so close to the surface only seconds ago, but it was no use. The little girl on the carousel had fled from her mind as quickly as she had entered.

A fire whistle wailing the end of another work day jarred her from her dazed reverie. Ashton supposed her questions would go unanswered forever. Still, she had been so close—or had she, she wondered.

Her head low, she walked back across the park, kicking at loose pebbles along the way. Whatever had triggered that one glimpse was gone, and nothing she could do could bring it back. Later, perhaps. No sense letting her inability to come up with a logical explanation for the strange sensation spoil her evening with Cav, she decided.

Four hours later, the *Wolf Lair* pickup was humming its way back to Fox Run. Ashton was certain that had she been a cat, she would have been purring loudly. She couldn't remember the last time she had enjoyed a date as much as she had the one she had just spent with Cav at *Billy Blalock's Blue Grass and Bar-B-Que* stuffing ribs and dancing cheek to cheek to country and western ballads.

Never before had she encountered a man who unknowingly had such a monopoly on raw virility. Everything about him exuded a primitive sensuality. No macho aftershave or other commercial product could ever come close to recreating the earthy mystique that Cav possessed.

Few words had been exchanged between them during the twenty-minute ride back from Hendersonville. There had been no need for conversation; they communicated with each other in the silence. Cav's very presence had a way of lulling every part of her mind and body into a mellow sweetness. With a satisfied sigh, she lay her head on his shoulder. Such moments came only once in a great while, and when they did, Ashton knew, the time was meant to be savored!

Cav veered off from Highway 64 onto the road that led up through the forest, explaining that no trip to Fox Run would be complete without a look at Connestee Falls by moonlight.

She could hardly get the words out of her mouth. "That sounds lovely." She tried to think of her work here in Fox Run, of the deposits of gallium she hoped to find, but nothing, not even thoughts of the research project, could still the hammering inside her chest.

A mile beyond the entranceway, Cav pulled off the road. "Mind a little walk?"

"Oh, no. Of course not," she assured him. There was a strange aching in her limbs that was becoming increasingly difficult to ignore. A walk was just what she needed.

Cav laced his fingers with hers, and together they walked out into the gray mist shrouding the forest. Overhead the stars were diamond studs twinkling on navy velvet. The air smelled of hickorywood. There was a tranquility in the forest that was almost spiritual.

With the icy sprays of Connestee Falls misting over them, they stood at the overlook and gazed up at the cascade of water crashing down onto the rocks. It was as though he could read her thoughts, for the moment she wished it he moved to close the short distance between them. He stepped toward her and then reached for her, pulling her closer, his eyes tracing her face, caressing it. Then his rock-hard chest and muscled arms imprisoned her. Blood pulsed dizzingly through her veins. A storm brewed inside her. The ache in her limbs had become a trembling she could not control.

It seemed forever before Cav's lips were on hers, but when his mouth reached its mark she drank greedily from it, and he answered her, gently at first and then with an eagerness and hunger that matched her own. He had whet a thirst in her that it seemed only he could quench. His caresses were wonderful and tormenting at the same time. His daring hands moved over her, lighting fires through her clothes where they traced her soft curves. The flesh beneath her Tartan wool jumper sizzled. She felt like a hot air balloon about to soar into the sky.

Ashton melted deeper and deeper against him. Her body was pliant and yielding; she was anxious to be molded to him in any way he saw fit. If only the intense longing growing inside her could be answered right then and there!

Chapter Four

Cav PULLED in behind Molly's station wagon and turned off the pickup's engine. "Okay, Cinderella," he said gently. "It's almost midnight."

Ashton raised her head from his shoulder. "Is my coach about to turn into a pumpkin?"

"No, but there's no guarantee I won't turn into a rat." His lips found their way back to hers.

His kisses were addictive. She would have been content to spend the rest of the night snuggled in his arms in the cab of the pickup. Sleep would be long in coming tonight, of that she was certain. Fantasies—about what might have happened between them up in the forest had the temperature not been below freezing—would keep her wide awake.

Molly sailed toward them the minute they stepped inside the door. "Sebastian's gone! I just know something dreadful has happened to him."

Cav caught her by the elbow. "Easy, Molly. We'll find the little bugger."

"He was all curled up by the hearth when I decided to go to the church social. When I got back, he had disappeared. I've checked all his hiding places. Dear me, what am I going to do without him?" she wailed, her hands wringing together.

Ashton sat the proprietress down at the telephone desk beside the staircase and gave her shoulder a pat of reassurance. "He probably just went for a prowl around

41

the neighborhood. He'll come back home when he gets hungry."

"He's too old to go tomcatting," whimpered Molly. Her chin dropped between her hands. "Oh, something terrible's happened to him. I just know it."

A faint meow sounded from behind the closed door opposite them.

"Sebastian must have decided to wait up for me," laughed Ashton, taking a few steps across the hall to her room.

The instant she cracked the door open, a ball of orange and black fur shot between her legs.

Molly flipflopped after him swatting the air at his tail. "Naughty boy," she shrilled. "I've been worried sick about you!"

Ashton pushed the door the rest of the way open. Her smile froze on her face and she sucked in her breath. The room looked like a tornado had ripped through it. Her suitcase had been turned upside down and its contents dumped haphazardly across the floor. File folders were scattered all across the bed, and the book she had been reading on the flight down was torn in two. It took several moments for the sight to sink in.

Cav came up behind to survey the damage. "Somehow, I don't think our friend Sebastian can be blamed for this." He gave her arm a comforting squeeze. "I'll call the police."

"Police? What's all this about calling the police?" asked Molly, shuffling past Cav. "Oh, dear me." Her face went ashen. Both hands shot up to her mouth. "I should have known something like this was bound to happen," she mumbled.

Ashton's brow arched questioningly. "What do you mean you should have known something like this was bound to happen?" she asked.

"I—I never lock my door. Not once during all these years." A tiny hand lifted to Ashton's face and stroked her cheeks gently. "I'm so sorry, dear."

"It wasn't your fault," she assured the old woman. "You couldn't help it." She'd be willing to bet that the inhabitants of Fox Run had boasted all their lives of living in a town where no one had to lock their doors.

Ashton took another look behind her. The room had been turned inside out, but why? What could the person who had searched here have possibly been after? Jewelry? Money? Ashton shivered. She felt as though the intruder had physically violated her. Nothing the police might do could change that!

Cav hung up the phone. "One of the officers is on his way over right now," he told them. "If I were you, Molly, I'd take stock of your jewelry, silver, money, and anything else that's small enough to be carried out easily."

Molly nodded. She climbed the stairs slowly, each step more labored than the last.

Ashton leaned against the bannister, her arms crossed and her face downcast. Why would anyone want to ransack her room? She was lucky that she had not left any of her valuables there. Poor Molly! She probably kept her life savings under her mattress.

Cav opened his arms wide, and Ashton came into them.

"Don't worry. We'll get to the bottom of this. I promise."

His arms formed a barricade around her. She smiled to herself. She didn't doubt for a moment that she was capable of getting to the bottom of it herself. Still, the "we" did have a nice ring to it, she decided as she snuggled close.

"Nothing's missing," said Molly as she came down the stairs a few minutes later.

"Are you certain?" asked Ashton, stunned by the announcement.

Molly nodded. "Positive. Everything's just the way I left it. My jewelry box was sitting right out on the bureau, and not a thing was out of place."

"I don't understand," frowned Cav.

Ashton was as baffled by Molly's findings as she was by the condition of her room. "Neither do I," she said thoughtfully. "Neither do I." Why should her room have been tossed and the others left untouched? Suddenly she froze. What if she had been singled out for this terrible act? But why, she wondered. Who could possibly want to harrass her? Aside from Molly and Cav, she hadn't exchanged more than five or ten minutes of conversation with anyone.

A knock sounded at the front door. Molly went to answer it. "Sergeant Kelly. Do come in," she told the officer.

The sergeant took off his cap and smoothed back the gray bristles of hair. "I understand you had a little problem here tonight."

Ashton answered for Molly. "That's right. Someone vandalized my room while I was out," she said, directing the way to her room.

The officer stuck a cigar in his mouth but didn't light it. "Somebody sure had a field day in here!" He flipped open his pad. "Name, please?" he asked Ashton.

"Ashton Paro. P-A-R-O."

The cigar rolled to the corner of his mouth. "Where you from, Miss Paro?"

"West Virginia. I'm visiting here for a few days," she volunteered in anticipation.

He kept writing. "We don't get many visitors up here."

"So I hear," she mumbled to herself.

"Anything missing?"

Ashton inventoried her belongings quickly. "Everything's here."

"All jewelry, credit cards, cash, traveler's checks accounted for?"

"Everything of any value was in my purse, and I had it with me," she answered.

Sergeant Kelly inspected the window, then the door. "No sign of forced entry. Anything jimmied out front?"

"The door wasn't locked," said Molly softly.

"Now you know better than that, Miz Siever." His syllables were as long and as drawn out as the shaking of his head. "Were you home all evening?" he asked Molly. His scribbling resumed; the professional tone had returned to his voice.

Molly shook her head. "I went down to the church along about eight to play bingo."

"What time did you get back?"

She sank against the door jamb. "I got back in time to watch the news on television, so it must have been around ten."

"Do you have any other guests?"

"Just Ashton."

He sucked harder on his cigar. "Did you notice anything unusual when you got home?"

Molly shook her head for the third time. " 'Fraid not."

The sergeant pointed his pencil at Ashton. "How about you, Miss Paro? Were you here all night?"

"I was out from about six until about fifteen minutes ago," she answered.

"You sure?"

She frowned. "Positive."

The officer's attention shifted back to Molly. "You didn't hear any noises coming from Miss Paro's room while she was gone, did you?"

"No, I didn't. And you don't have to raise your voice with me, Grady Kelly. I'm not deaf, you know," she snapped.

He closed his pad and slipped it back into his pocket. "Then I'd say the intruder entered between eight and ten when the house was empty." He seemed pleased with his deduction. "Most likely, what we have here is the work of some Halloween prankster. Since nothing was taken, I wouldn't be too upset, Miss Paro." He tipped his cap in her direction. "Just sorry you had to be the one inconvenienced. Things like this aren't good for public relations." He walked back out into the foyer.

"And that's that?" asked Ashton. "You think that mess was caused by kids looking for a good time?"

"That's my professional opinion, m'am."

Ashton felt the hair on the back of her neck bristle. "Perhaps you could explain, then, why my room was the only one selected for their mischief, or why nothing there or anywhere else in the house was taken?"

He curled the tip of his moustache. "That's got me stumped, too."

She positioned herself between him and the door. "So what are you going to do about it?"

"Alright, Miss Paro, if it'll make you sleep any easier, I'll wake up a few of the neighbors and ask them if they saw anything out of the ordinary going on over here tonight." He sidestepped past her. "Give me a call down at the station in the morning. Maybe I'll have some answers for you then."

"Thank you. I would appreciate that very much."

Cav joined her on the porch. They watched as the squad car rolled down the street to the next house and stopped.

Cav wrapped his arm around her waist. "It doesn't make any sense at all."

"No, it doesn't." Ashton ran her hand through the mane of ringlets covering her neck. Then again, she thought, having her room ransacked while the rest of the house remained untouched wasn't the first strange thing to have happened to her in the past twelve hours. She hadn't expected Welcome Wagon, but she certainly hadn't anticipated the kind of reception she had been given thus far. It seemed that Cav and Molly were the only two people who hadn't treated her as if she were an intruder.

Cav kissed the top of her head. "We'll sort all this out tomorrow. Right now, you'd better try and get some sleep."

"I'm afraid my eyes will have to close in shifts tonight."

His eyes connected with hers through the darkness. "I understand the security is excellent at that new resort I told you about."

Strong arms encircled her when she nodded her acceptance of his offer.

Molly walked up behind them. "I think that's a splendid idea, Cav." She took Ashton by the arm and led her over to the swing. "Let's face it, honey. What the sergeant said is a crock of malarkey! Kids around here don't do anything

worse than race their cars down Main Street on Saturday
night."

"What's your explanation?"

Molly hesitated. She glanced over at Cav. "Well, I didn't
want to say anything around the men, but I think there's a
kook running around town. I've heard stories about other
incidents." She picked up the rosebud pendant dangling
around Ashton's neck and held it up to the light. "How
pretty." She dropped it back down. "I don't mean to alarm
you, but I think this fellow saw you when you came into
town and might have been following you ever since," she
said in a voice that could barely be heard. "Maybe this was
his way of letting you know that he's keeping his eye on
you."

Ashton thought for a moment. "I guess that makes
about as much sense as any of the other theories."

"More. Now you run along with Cav," she ordered.
"Just knowing you were in his protection would ease my
mind considerably."

Ashton tried hard not to smile. She wouldn't hurt
Molly's feelings for anything in the world, but she had
never considered herself to be someone who needed to be
protected and she wasn't about to start now. Still, if protective custody involved Cav as her guardian, the thought
was very tempting. Only one thing troubled her. "What
about you?" she asked her elderly friend. "If there is some
weirdo on the prowl, you shouldn't be here alone."

"It wasn't my room that was ransacked!" With that, she
linked her arm through Ashton's. "I don't see that you
have any choice in the matter. I've just evicted you!"

An hour later, Ashton sat deep in an easy chair with a
snifter of brandy in her hand. Cav's German shepherd,
Zebo, stood guard beside her. Cav had called his place a
cabin. She certainly hadn't expected to find a century-old
manor with spiral ceilings, pegged oak floors, and chest-
nut rafters! The living room alone was five times the size
of her whole apartment. What hunt parties the manor's
original owners must have hosted there!

Cav sat perched on the arm of her chair. Her eye caught the way his chest rose and fell with each breath he took. Ashton knew that the brandy he was giving her was not responsible for the wild beating of her heart or for the butterflies in her stomach.

"Another?" offered Cav when her goblet was empty.

She shook her head. "No, thank you. One's enough."

"Are you sure? It's guaranteed to keep the bogeyman away."

Her eyes sought his, her pulse pounding. "I thought that was your job."

"You're right. It is." He pulled her to her feet and molded her close.

Ashton felt as if Cav were an artist and she his piece of clay. His fingers were bold and imaginative; his hands were shaping her shoulder blades, her waist, her hips, her buttocks in any way they desired.

His mouth pressed her lips and she felt the wet, demanding heat of it. His tongue pushed between her teeth and darted into every recess of her mouth, tracing its softness, caressing it, telegraphing electric messages that spread like shock waves through her body. Her stomach catapulted into her throat. Each breath she drew was but a gasp. Each and every cell was ignited in a blaze that Ashton could barely keep under control.

Their passage up the stairs seemed to take forever. Finally, Ashton found herself standing beside his bed. She couldn't speak; she could barely breathe. She could only hope that her eyes would relay to him the messages her mind and heart were sending.

Wools on top of mohair on top of tweed piled onto the floor. Her heart somersaulted with each addition to the mound of clothes. At last, wisps of silks and satins swished down her legs, and she stood naked before him. At that instant, all she wanted was to be completely sated by him. Adventurous fingers made bold by the quakings inside her became lost in the rug of dark curls that carpeted his chest.

She closed her eyes, her thoughts leaping beyond to what lay ahead. She didn't need to open her eyes to know as her hands traced his body that he was every bit as fine a male specimen as she had imagined.

In one quick, easy motion, Cav swept her off the floor and onto the bed. His eyes raked her, tracing the route his hands would soon take. Then his gaze became gentle, as though she were some precious objet d'art to be revered and adored.

"You're beautiful," he whispered, lowering his head to nuzzle the soft, fleshy mounds whose peaks were rising at the very touch of his breath. "Exquisite!"

Ashton was so busy trying to commit to memory each detail of his finely sculpted face that she could do little more than moan a reply.

He canopied her like a welcomed blanket on a cold night. The gleam in his eyes was made feral by the moonlight filtering into the room through the pines. But his touch was far from savage. Gentle hands caressed her breasts' fullness. Rosy nipples stood at attention under his mouth's teasing inspection. Kisses trailed down her ribs, across her stomach, over her trembling belly. His tongue paused to slowly taste her navel and then moved lower to probe softer depths. Her heart plunged to the very spot it had awakened.

Cav studied the territory diligently before staking his claim. Not one inch of her quaking body went unexplored. "Oh, Ashton, I want you to want me as much as I do you," he mumbled between her silken thighs.

"I do, Cav. I swear I do." Her voice shook. She pulled his full weight down upon her. She wanted to belong to him; she wanted him to take possession of what was his.

His gentleness forgotten in his urgency, he sandwiched her against the bed. Limbs tangled together, and hearts raced in unison. Their bodies and souls were bridged.

Blood flowed freely from his veins to hers, warming her and chilling her at the same time.

His thrusts were powerful, and she clung to him for salvation. Every stroke was received and returned with an eagerness that knew no limits and no shame. Her need shattered his. His all but paralyzed hers.

Like old lovers, each was attuned to the other's wants and needs. Nothing went unshared. Their union was a meeting of the souls and a joining of the minds. Cav strove to lavish her with more pleasure than she had ever thought possible, and she knew she would settle for nothing less for him. He guided the rise and fall of her every breath as naturally as the moon takes charge of the oceans' tides. Never had she imagined such total bliss. With a breathtaking onslaught that one minute was lustfully savage and the next minute was infinitely gentle, Cav carried Ashton further and further away on a cloud of euphoria.

Ashton awoke a few hours later, trembling. She had escaped the dancing demons at her feet none too soon. A moment longer and she would have gone up in flames, a human sacrifice.

Cav's arms were quick to comfort her. "You alright, sweetheart?"

"Just a bad dream," she told him, whispering. "Go back to sleep."

With a promise to ward off all bogeymen, whether real or imagined, Cav gathered her as close as he could.

Her eyes remained glued to the rafters long after he had drifted back into slumber. She was afraid to go back to sleep. She had just fought her way out of a nightmare, the same nightmare that had plagued her during childhood and had made her cry every time the lights were turned off and she was left alone. The dream had not returned since her last year in high school. From then on, she had not dreaded sleep. Why should the nightmare suddenly recur, she wondered. Had the merry-go-round in the park triggered more than just a glimpse of herself as a little girl? She finally found the courage to close her eyes, but she knew that sleep would be long in coming.

Chapter Five

DAYLIGHT broke across the sky in rosy streamers and trickled into the bedroom. Ashton arched and stretched like a contented cat awakening from its nap. She had decided an hour ago to put the nightmare behind her. After all, she was a grown woman now, and the fears her mind concocted should no longer be allowed to bully her.

The man lying next to her was proof that the best part of last night had been real. She and Cav had consumed each other with a hungry passion that knew no inhibitions, and as her thoughts drifted back over the night just passed, everything else, including the nightmare, became insignificant in comparison.

Ashton tucked her curves closer to his. She smiled to herself. It would be unfair to deprive him of any part of her. She counted the sun freckles sprinkled across his nose. If only she had the power to command time to stand still! How wonderful it would be to revel in his nearness a little while longer. Her eyes did not stray from his face. She didn't want to miss the slightest twitch. Perhaps there was some truth to an old Apache saying she had once heard: if you gaze on someone while he's sleeping, your souls would be bound together for eternity. She angled herself closer and stared harder and longer in hopes of willing it true.

Cav awakened to fingertips grazing on the dark stubble shadowing his face. "Any regrets?"

"Only one." She did her best to keep a poker face. "Had I known then what I know now, I would definitely have rooted for the *Dolphins*. No doubt about it!"

Warm legs wound around her. "And had I known you were sitting in the stands, I would have dragged you down to the locker room and ravaged you right then and there." To prove his point, he soldered her lips with a kiss that was as hot as the pressure building in his thighs.

Fingers teasing deliciously down her body rekindled fire on top of fire en route. Marble-hard nipples danced at attention inside his flaming mouth and then rose exquisitely higher as his head moved lower and they were exposed, wet, to the cool morning air.

Ashton felt as though she were on the verge of being completely short-circuited. Her words were but gurgles in her throat, but he had no trouble interpreting the instructions she gave. He guided himself to his mark amid sweet gasps and sighs of delight. Nothing held back, their bodies came together in one fantastic surge of ecstasy. He had memorized her well. Every billow and swell were perfectly timed. Each movement was synchronized with the last and with the one to come.

Cav drove himself deeper and deeper home. Backs arched; limbs gripped, fingers dug into flesh. Ashton knew she could not contain herself much longer. She held onto him for dear life. He was her float, and she clung to him with all her might as wave after wave broke over her.

The exact tempo to orchestrate their symphony was found at last. Total contentment saturated them. Ashton was certain that none of the great maestros could have inspired such harmony.

She nudged him a few minutes later. "Don't get too comfortable, buster. I hear this establishment serves breakfast in bed."

His arms refused to uncage her. "That was the main course, madame."

"Is that any way to talk to *Wolf Lair*'s first guest?" she teased, trying to wiggle out of his hold.

He rolled over her and pinned her shoulders to the mattress. "Don't be difficult with me, lady, or I'll—"

"You'll what?"

He swung himself over her and onto the floor. "Or I'll use all the hot water, and you'll have to shiver in the shower."

Ashton reclined on her elbows and kicked away the covers. "I believe I know of a way that will allow enough hot water for both of us."

Cav's eyes feasted on her as though he were seeing her for the first time. "You do, do you?"

"Mmm, and conserve energy as well." She came off the bed and did a few ballet stretches for his benefit before taking his robe from his closet and slipping it on. "Remember the motto of the sixties? Save water, shower together?"

He hooked his arm around hers. "Who am I to deny my guests whatever pleasures their hearts desire?"

The temptation to cocoon themselves back inside the stack of quilts was too difficult to resist. When they finally emerged nearly an hour later, they showered quickly—and separately—donned jeans and ski sweaters and raced down the stairs before another moment of weakness overcame them.

Ashton admired the kitchen from the doorway before she entered it. Facing out over a lake, the room looked as though it had just been lifted from the pages of *House Beautiful.* Sunlight entered through windows that were long and wide and bounced off tiles that were the color of desert sand. In the center of the room was a huge butcher-block worktable, and hanging above it was enough copper cookware to equip a gourmet restaurant. This certainly was not the rough cabin kitchen she had expected before she arrived at *Wolf's Lair.*

Ashton walked inside for a better look. "I had no idea that dishwashers were in vogue at the turn of the century."

Cav poured two glasses of orange juice and handed one

to her. "There's a lot to be said for indoor plumbing and electricity."

"I thought you were the kind of man who enjoys roughing it," she teased.

"I do, but my guests deserve comfort." He clicked his glass against hers. "Here's to *Wolf Lair's* first guest."

"And to the the host with the most."

"I aim to please!" He downed his juice in one swallow. "Alright, pretty lady, what would suit your fancy for breakfast?"

She was tempted to answer with his name, but knowing how much work was involved in her preliminary survey, she decided against it. She could not remember ever having had to remind herself that work took precedence over fun! "Why don't you surprise me?" she said, pulling a stool up to the worktable.

He dropped a kiss on her nose. "How about eggs, home fries, country ham, and biscuits?"

"Are we dieting?" She patted his stomach. It was as hard as the cast-iron skillet he had just set on the stove. "What can I do to help?"

"Not one thing! Just sit back and enjoy the view." He pushed up the sleeves of his sweater. "Chef Cavanaugh is about to prepare a breakfast that will put the golden arches of McDonald's to shame."

She fixed herself a cup of tea and did just as he had suggested. She found her view of the chef as he worked in his kitchen to be just as nice as the view of the sloping acres outside. Cav's skill as a cook amazed her. She smiled to herself. Some men felt that any show of culinary talent would emasculate them. It certainly didn't make Cav look any less masculine!

"Where's your phone?" she asked after the tray of biscuits had been slid into the oven. "I have to catch some people in their offices this morning."

Cav got a half-dozen eggs out of the refrigerator. "In the study. First door on the left past the stairs."

"Bad news?" he asked when she returned.

"I just spoke with Sergeant Kelly." The frown did not leave her face. "It seems that none of Molly's neighbors noticed anything suspicious last night." She slumped against the wall. "He told me that he's more convinced than ever that I was the butt of a Halloween prank."

"Sounds like he doesn't want to admit that he's stumped." Cav took her hand and led her into a nook that was just big enough for a table for two. "Just don't you worry! There won't be a repeat performance up here," he assured her with a kiss on the cheek. "Not as long as Zebo and I have anything to do with it."

Ashton bit her tongue. What harm was there in letting him think she needed her own personal knight in shining armor?

He returned from the kitchen with two plates heaped high with food. "Ta-tumm! Is this a feast fit for a king?"

Ashton picked up her fork, but she didn't know quite where to start. "I had no idea we were consuming the day's allotment of calories all in one meal."

"The way I figure it, we'll have all day to burn them off." He pulled up a chair beside her. "What you said about espionage being a common practice among rival mining companies started me thinking," he remarked between bites. "Do you think it's possible that one of your competitors had you followed to Fox Run with plans of getting you off the job and them taking over?"

"Possible, but not probable." She paused to butter her biscuit. "I had the same thought last night, so I checked with North Carolina's Office of Natural Resources in Raleigh a little while ago. They informed me that *Consolidated* is the only mining company that's expressed interest in western North Carolina for several years now."

Cav stopped eating. "That's the only explanation that would have made any sense to me."

His observation echoed her own thoughts. Had another company been involved, she could have rationalized the reason. Even had robbery been the motive, she wouldn't have felt so unsettled about the whole thing. But as it was, the person responsible for ransacking her room had done so out of reasons that were as yet known only to him. That in itself was almost as terrifying as her nightmare.

"I have a great idea," announced Cav a few minutes later.

"What's that?" She knew he was trying to cheer her up, so she decided to let him think he was succeeding. There was no point letting her worries ruin his day.

He reached for a second helping. "Why don't you call *Consolidated* in a few days and tell them you suspect that the eastern slope of Bear Wallow contains an even higher concentration of gallium than the western one?"

She rested her chin on her hands. "Why would I want to do something like that?"

"So you can extend your stay, of course." He drowned his biscuit in redeye gravy. "Seems to me they'd be all too eager to have you make friends with the owner."

Her mood began to lift. "You're forgetting one little detail."

"What's that?"

"Your side of Bear Wallow has no gallium at all." Her arms crossed under her chest. A mischievous gleam twinkled in her eyes. "Tell me something. If there were gallium deposits on your property, would you let us mine it?"

Cav answered without hesitation. "Not a chance. I like my side of the mountain just the way it is." He flashed her one of those crooked smiles that had become so familiar to her. "Of course, I wouldn't offer too much opposition if you tried to strike a bargain with me."

"What kind of a bargain?" Ashton felt a smile coming on.

"Your favors in exchange for my gallium," he said in all seriousness.

"You've already had my favors, remember?" She laughed. There was no doubt about who was responsible for her good mood!

Cav pushed back from the table. "What say we take the

horses out for a ride? Nothing's prettier than a mountain coming to life in the morning."

"Don't you have a resort to build?" she asked as she began to clear away the dishes. "I certainly wouldn't want my presence to interfere with your daily routine."

"Who says this isn't my daily routine?" he asked, taking a nip at her neck. "I always prowl the courthouse the last Monday of the month in search of unsuspecting female geologists, lure them up to my mountain, ply them with home cooking, and force them to indulge in my fantasies."

Ashton felt a twinge of jealousy tugging at her smile. She knew he was teasing. Still, she couldn't help but envy any woman who had preceded her in his bed. This man had, without a doubt, perfected lovemaking to an art. Of course there had been other women in his life, she told herself.

His lips brushed away her musings. "Besides, the horses need the exercise."

"What? Oh, yes, the horses do need exercising." She couldn't help but chuckle. "Not to mention us!"

"Then you'll go?"

"Love to," she replied. "I'll even take along my pack and start collecting rock samples along the way."

"Fair enough." Cav began loading the dishwasher. "By the way, I'm sending a few of the guys over to Asheville late this afternoon to pick up some plumbing supplies. If you'd like, they can take your car and return it to the airport for you. You're more than welcome to use one of *Wolf Lair's* vehicles."

Ashton considered his offer. She knew what her answer would be without giving it a second thought. Apparently, he took it for granted that she would remain with him for the duration of her study. She certainly wouldn't want to disappoint him! "Sid will love that idea," she said, trying to keep a straight face.

Cav straightened. "Sid? Who's he?"

She was certain she detected a jealous note in his tone.

"Sid's my boss. He's always growling about the expense tabs I run up when I'm out on assignment."

"Maybe he'll be so grateful he'll let you stay a few days longer." He pushed her away from the counter. "Now that that's settled, why don't you go up and get your gear together?"

"You're sure a quick ride won't delay you?" she asked on her way out.

"Why, Miss Paro, are you propositioning me?" he teased.

"On the horses, silly!" She ran up the stairs, happier than she had been in a long time. Her assignment was turning out to be a vacation after all. She had Cav to thank for that!

A short while later, with Zebo in the cab between them, they arrived at the stable that had been built to house two dozen horses. Only two of the stalls were occupied. Cav led both of the horses out.

"Take your pick," he told her.

She studied her choices. The brown mare whinnied softly. "How can I resist? I'll take her." She took hold of the lead rope. "What's her name?"

"Calandre," he answered. He led the palomino over to a post and tied him up. "And this handsome fellow is Fancy Dancy."

Ashton fed them each a sugar cube that she had brought from the house. "A little bribery never hurts," she grinned, scratching their noses.

Cav started grooming his horse. "You won't need it with these two. They're both very well mannered."

"Just like their owner," she laughed, picking up the body brush.

"You got it!"

"I love to ride," she said as she brushed Calandre. "I used to keep a horse at a friend's stable, but eventually I had to sell him. I only had time to ride on the weekends, and some weeks I couldn't even manage that."

"They need a lot of TLC." He flashed her a quick grin as he bent down to pick Fancy's hooves. "Just like us people."

She tacked Calandre up a few minutes later. "Trail rides through these mountains would certainly be a big tourist draw," she remarked, fitting the bit into the mare's mouth.

Cav adjusted his leathers. "You don't think I'd be a big enough draw on my own?"

She swung herself up into the saddle. "Maybe for one or two of the weaker sex." Laughing, she nudged her horse forward.

Riding side by side, they headed down the hill on a loose rein. The countryside was just awakening, and as Cav had promised, nothing was prettier than a mountain coming to life after a night's sleep. The fog that wreathed the pinnacles of Wolf Mountain and Bear Wallow evaporated slowly. Arrows of light danced like sparkling gems across the frost-laced meadows.

They picked up the rein and began to trot across hills that rose and fell beneath them.

"This is fantastic!" exclaimed Ashton. With her hair streaming a trail of curls behind her, she felt as free as the wind that was whistling past her cheeks. "I can't think of a more invigorating way to start the day."

"Thanks a lot, pal!" Cav gave Fancy a kick and raced in front of her.

Ashton followed close behind. Calandre's canter was like the movement of a giant rocking horse.

"There's a log across the path just ahead," he called out. "She's as fine a jumper as you'll find anywhere."

Ashton could feel the adrenaline start pumping inside her. Nothing made a rider feel so much in control as jumping his mount. The log in view, she leaned forward in her seat and steered Calandre right toward the center of it. Her legs were clamped on the mare's sides. Her hands were lowered close on her neck. Ashton held her breath. She was aware of the great strength underneath her. With all the grace and poise of a seasoned hunter, Calandre stretched out and sailed over the log.

"Good girl," praised Ashton, giving her mount a hearty pat.

"I don't remember you making such a fuss over me," teased Cav.

"Next time I will. I promise," she said, trotting up alongside him. She was surprised that the butterflies returned to her stomach at the very thought.

"Just don't forget, or I'll have to remind you," he told her as they crossed the creek.

Ashton smiled to herself. She was certain she wouldn't have to be reminded. She was already looking forward to the next time Cav made love to her.

Cav turned the horses towards the construction trailer. "You're one hell of a rider, you know that?"

"You're not so bad yourself," she returned laughingly.

"If everything's under control at the site, we'll ride on up to the ridge," he suggested.

"Great! I'm anxious to start work on my preliminary survey as soon as I can."

"I'm anxious for you to get started, too," he announced with a grin. "The sooner you get all this work behind you, the more time you'll have for me."

Smiling, Ashton sat deeper into the saddle. She wasn't about to object! If she were lucky, there would be sufficient gallium deposits on Bear Wallow to warrant a full-scale investigation. She wouldn't mind that at all.

Chapter Six

Ashton pointed to a cream-colored Mercedes parked beside the trailer. "If that's the car you offered to put at my disposal, I accept!"

"Dream on." Cav booted Fancy forward. "Bet you can't guess who it belongs to."

"Bet I can." She wondered why seeing it there would make her feel so glum. Maybe it was because of the way Breyer had cross-examined her yesterday. She hoped that interrogating newcomers was not on his list of things to do today. "What do you suppose he wants?" she wondered aloud; already, she could feel her body tensing.

"Only one way to find out," answered Cav, picking up the rein.

Even though she was too far away to distinguish the details of Breyer's face, she knew his eyes were on her. She could sense their intensity. Myra's warning echoed inside her head. She knew she'd never be able to look at him again without being reminded of the waitress's words of caution. Yet he seemed harmless. His bark was probably worse than his bite.

As she neared the construction office, Ashton could see that her gut feeling was right. Breyer was staring at her. His look, however, was one of curiosity, not one of offense. It was apparent that he had not expected to find her there. After all, she had mentioned something yesterday about having plans to stay at the Red Fox Inn. What Molly had implied about him being a ladies' man made her chuckle. He seemed far too austere for that!

Ashton kept her eyes on him. She could see that he was not alone. Standing next to him was a woman who was dressed in an all-gray ensemble of hat, coat, and boots. Her hat was aslant over one eye. Breyer's friend had a rather worldly air about her, and it seemed to Ashton that she couldn't be a Fox Run resident.

She and Cav dismounted at the drive leading into the office and walked the horses the rest of the way in. Ashton noticed that Breyer said something to his companion and pointed to the car. Then, he began walking down the drive to meet them. Cav called out to him and told him to wait, but Breyer kept walking in their direction.

"Sorry to disturb you, Cav," he said after a few pleasant exchanges with them both. "I seem to have come at the wrong time. I'll come back later."

"No problem," Cav assured him. "I had to stop by the trailer anyway to check with Bud."

"I brought over a contract for you to review," explained Breyer, standing in front of the horses. "Have a look at it sometime this week. No hurry. Get back to me when you can."

His friend had walked over to join them. She ignored Breyer's assurance that he was ready to leave and walked right past him.

"I'm Judith Breyer. Hamp's sister," she said to Cav.

Cav introduced himself, then Ashton.

Her gloved hands remained folded at her waist. "Ashton. . . . Lovely name. Have we met before? Last year, perhaps?"

Ashton shook her head. "I don't live here. I'm just visiting."

"My mistake," she said cheerfully. "I was watching you galloping across the field. You ride beautifully. Such a good seat."

"Thank you." Even though Judith had a self-indulgent look about her, she struck Ashton as being the personable member of the family. She was certainly much friendlier than her brother.

Ashton glanced at Breyer. He and Cav were engrossed in conversation, but he still managed to keep one eye on her. "Do you ride?" she asked Judith, sensing that the woman wanted to talk. The two of them walked on in front of the men.

"I used to when I was younger but not any more. Once I hit forty, I found that my instinct for self-preservation prevented me from taking any unnecessary risks. Riding can be very dangerous, you know," she added as an afterthought.

Ashton was quick to agree. "Then again, when you get into an automobile, you're taking your life into your hands."

"That's true." Judith tucked a stray wisp of hair back under her hat. "Cav's idea of a ski resort here is really quite marvelous. I can't wait until it opens."

"You sound like a skier."

"I'm not." She frowned suddenly. "As a matter of fact, I'm not very keen on anything that can put me in a hospital." Her perfectly made-up face was aglow with smiles the next minute. "Think of all the people who'll come here to ski. Fox Run's entire social scene may be changed."

Ashton chuckled. She had no idea Fox Run had a social scene to begin with.

"You know, this is such a dreadful little town," Judith continued. "If Hamp didn't insist on staying here, I'd never come back to visit even though I was born here."

They arrived at the trailer, Ashton tied Calandre to a shrub. "You don't live here?" she asked Judith.

Judith's eyes rolled back dramatically. "Heavens, no. I had enough of being a country bumpkin when I was growing up. I prefer bright lights and big cities!"

Breyer took his sister by the arm a few minutes later. "Come along, Judith. I doubt Toxaway Inn will hold our breakfast reservation much longer."

His sister brushed away his hand in much the same

manner as she would have shooed away an annoying bug. "Good luck with your resort, Cav. I think it's a splendid idea." She turned to Ashton, her face all smiles. "And it was so lovely meeting you, dear. Perhaps we can get together for lunch sometime. I'll call you," she said before being ushered away.

"Hey boss, you got a phone call," blared a hearty voice from inside the trailer.

Cav tied his horse alongside Calandre. "Come on in," he told Ashton. "Won't be but a sec." He took her arm and led her inside. On his way over to the desk, he hurriedly introduced her to a big blond hulk who could easily have passed for Paul Bunyan. "Ashton Paro, I'd like you to meet my foreman, Bud Marlow. Bud, Ashton."

"From what I hear, you're the backbone of this project," said Ashton, her voice friendly.

Bud grinned. "I could tell you a few tales about him, too." He handed her a styrofoam cup. "How 'bout some coffee? Just perked it myself."

"Thanks."

Bud peered through the window, watching as the Mercedes rolled down the road. "Strange pair," he mumbled under his breath.

"Yes, they are," she agreed. Judith was the friendlier of the two by far, but there was still something a little peculiar about her. Still, she seemed to be quite a match for her brother. She was probably one of the few people in western North Carolina who could put him in his place when he got too stuffy, decided Ashton.

"Their mama was a real looney-tune," continued Bud, helping himself to another cup of coffee. "But now, ol' Doc Breyer was as nice a man as you'd ever hope to find. Real down to earth. Too bad some of his niceness didn't rub off on his young 'uns."

Cav hung up the phone. "Charley Ferris is coming over to inspect the wiring over at the hotel," he told Bud.

Bud threw on his jacket. "I'll get up there and make sure everything's all set for him, boss."

"Thanks, Bud." He turned to Ashton. "Sorry, babe, but I'm going to have to take a rain check on that ride. I've been after Ferris since the first of October to get his fanny up here and inspect the electrical work."

"No problem," she returned, smiling. "Like I told you before, I don't want my being here to interfere with the resort."

He folded her to his chest. "It already has. But that's my fault, not yours."

She wondered why her stomach always did somersaults when he pulled her close.

"I know you've got your work cut out for you, too," he said, releasing her, "so if you want to go on and take Calandre up to Bear Wallow, that's fine with me. The land's posted against trespassers so you'll have the place all to yourself."

"Seeing as how I'm one myself I believe I'll take you up on that." She chuckled and slipped her knapsack back over her arms. "All you have to do is point me in the right direction," she said as they walked outside.

Cav gave her a leg-up into the saddle and ran his hand down her calf before tightening the girth. "Just stick to the logging trail. It'll take you right where you want to go." He handed her the reins. "Why don't you take Zebo along? He's great at chasing away catamounts. You sure you got everything you need in your pack?"

Ashton turned Calandre towards the ridge. "If I don't I'll send Zebo back down with a list of what I need."

Cav walked her down to the road. "I should be through with Charley about one. Think you'd have time for the grand tour by then?"

"It's a date." She whistled for Zebo, then booted Calandre into a trot.

It took nearly half an hour before she reached the top of the ridge. Once there, Ashton halted and gave the horse a loose rein. She surveyed with interest the hive-like activity of men and machinery in the valley below. Up until then, she had no idea how vast an area the *Wolf Lair* proj-

ect encompassed. East of her were the bungalow hide-
aways that made up the hotel. The ski slopes were to the
west, and beyond the woods to the north was the hunting
lodge where Cav lived. She could see that he had gone to
great lengths to blend his resort with the natural lay of the
land. He had used nature to provide the perfect backdrop
for the scene he had created.

Cav had been right, she decided as she turned Calandre
across the ridge. Wolf Mountain was like no other place
she had ever seen. This truly was God's country.

Ashton frisked her horse across the crest and onto Bear
Wallow. No wonder Cav didn't want his land mined, she
thought, taking one last look behind her. She wouldn't,
either, if she owned it. Man could add nothing to the splendor that already existed there. There was nothing to im-
prove on. Mother Nature had seen to that!

Well into Bear Wallow, Ashton gave the horse a rest and
checked her maps. The greatest concentration of gallium
supposedly lay southwest of the point where she was.

She rode a few miles farther until she came to the land-
mark she had red-inked on her map. There at the sawmill
camp was where her investigation would begin. Just north
of that should be the highest density of the metal she was
seeking.

Ashton left Calandre grazing below the limb where she
was tied. After hooking a pedometer to her belt, she gave a
whistle for Zebo and set out on foot to explore the land
north of the mill.

The sheet of marble-like stone she was looking for was
eight-tenths of a mile beyond the sawmill camp. The satellite sweep of the area had pinpointed the gallium in the
same general location. She slipped out of her knapsack and
sat down on the outcropping where she began chiseling the
first layer in search of the black arteries that would signal
the gallium's presence.

The sound of leaves crackling made Ashton shoot
straight up. She whirled around with her pick poised as a
weapon. Before she could grab hold of Zebo's collar, the

shepherd went bounding into the bushes with his ears standing at attention. He returned a few minutes later with a whimper.

"Must have been one of those bobcats, hey, boy?" She gave his head a pat, then settled back down at her work. One eye remained peeled at the brush in case the catamount decided to show more spunk.

It was past noon before she hiked back down to the mill. Weighting down Calandre's saddlebags were enough rock samples to provide the information she needed. From them, she could chart the location for tomorrow's work.

Ashton headed Calandre back down the logging road with Zebo following close on their heels. Midway down, she spotted a waterfall in the distance and cut through the woods to investigate.

A few minutes later, she sat tall in her saddle and enjoyed the cascade below her. The sound of water roiling down the mountainside was relaxing, the sort of noise she could easily unwind to after a hard day at the office. Ashton smiled. It was even more soothing than a wine spritzer. She inhaled several deep breaths. The air was thick with the smell of balsam. Ashton snapped a picture of the waterfall with her camera. There was a lot to be said for getting back to nature, she decided. She promised herself that in the future she would take more time from her hectic schedule to do just that. She wondered how much time she had left until her next vacation leave. *Wolf Lair* was the perfect place for that R-and-R she had coming.

A sound like that of a car backfiring pierced the mountain's tranquility. Calandre cantered a few steps, then began dancing in place.

"Easy, babe," cooed Ashton, though her own heart was pounding. "It's okay. Nothing's going to hurt you." She gave the mare's neck a pat when she obeyed her command to stand. "Good, girl."

Ashton whistled for Zebo. He came bounding up behind them. She scanned every tree around them. The noise had sounded suspiciously like a rifle shot. The land was posted. Cav, himself, had told her that.

A second shot rang out. This one was even closer. Calandre spooked. Her head jerked back and rammed Ashton in the chest. Ashton lost the reins. Calandre reared straight up. All the mare's weight was on her hind legs. Her front legs struck out at the air in front of her.

Ashton grabbed hold of the mane and braced herself against the horse's neck. Her only hope of getting all four legs back onto the ground was to shift the weight from the back to the front. She tried not to think of what might happen if the horse lost its balance and fell to the ground with her on its back.

"Easy, girl. Easy. Just calm down." She did her best to keep her voice soft and even. A horse could sense the fear of its rider. If Calandre lost confidence in her, they could both take a flying leap into the ravine.

Ashton prayed no more shots would ring out. She could feel the tension gradually drain from the mare. A few minutes later the horse was standing in place and waiting for the next command as if nothing had happened at all.

Ashton booted the horse back onto the logging road. She kept her moving along energetically until she came to the ridge. There, she trotted across onto *Wolf Lair* property. When the construction site was in view, she pulled the mare around and turned for a look behind her. The thought of her close call up on Bear Wallow Mountain chilled her blood.

Chapter Seven

ASHTON led Calandre back into her stall. The horse seemed to have forgotten all about what had happened up on Bear Wallow. Ashton wished she could erase it as easily from her own mind. She still felt shaky, and just thinking about the horse rearing up with her made her feel even more squeamish.

She just couldn't seem to figure any of it out, no matter how hard she tried. The rifle had been fired from close range. Surely the person aiming it had spotted them. After seeing the horse spook, why on earth would he have fired a second shot? None of it made any sense, she decided, as she filled Calandre's feed bucket with an extra scoop of oats.

Just as she finished currying her horse, a hearty voice came from behind. "How was your ride?"

She turned around and smiled. Cav's voice could calm the worst of the rogue horses, yet the sound of it had so far never failed to cause her heart to stop, start, and sputter all in the same motion.

"It would have been perfect had it not been for some fool hunter shooting at anything that moved," she replied.

His forehead creased. "Damn! Those poachers sure are getting brazen, going out in broad daylight. Did Calandre give you any trouble?"

She patted the horse's side. "She got a little jittery, but nothing I couldn't handle."

71

Cav leaned against the stall. A sly grin crooked his lips. "I bet there's not much you couldn't handle."

"Not much," she winked. She closed the gap between them. Her body hungered for the steel-hard feel of his. Her thumbs hooked into his belt loops. "Too bad you couldn't have gone out with us. We came across some real cozy little pine bowers."

His hands grasped her buttocks and pulled her against him. "But then you wouldn't have gotten any work done!"

"All work and no play make geologists very dull company," she said, winding her arms around his neck.

Cav turned and pinned her against the wall. Again his tongue probed her mouth with an intoxicating sweetness. "Too bad there's not a carpet of fresh hay in here," he mumbled, his lips on hers and his voice thick. His eyes were glazed with desire.

Ashton nipped at his lips. Her tongue polished his teeth. "And whose fault is that, may I ask?"

"I take full responsibility." His powerful hands slipped under her sweater. His warm fingers diligently worked open the hooks of her bra, and, freed from their lacy bindings, the soft, silken mounds he sought sprang out to greet him. "Umm. Too bad Sarah's up at the house."

Ashton said nothing.

Cav held her out at arm's length. "What's the matter? Aren't you the least bit curious about Sarah?"

Her finger anchored suggestively on his belt buckle. "I'm not the jealous type." She broke into a smile. "Besides, the way I figure it, after you've had the best, why should you call in the second string?"

"Good point." He grinned. "Just in case you're interested, Sarah's Bud's wife. She comes in a few times a week to clean up after me."

Ashton ran a fingernail along his chest, tracing it through his shirt. "That's too bad. All this time I thought you had burned your jockstrap and had become a totally liberated male."

"Disappointed?" His forefinger skied the course from

her throat to her belly button. She sucked in her breath as his finger lingered there, gently tickling.

"Actually, I'm relieved," she said with a sigh when he took away his hand. "You almost had me convinced you were perfect." But she couldn't breathe deeply for long. His fingers had moved up and were teasing her nipples; Ashton was beginning to gasp for breath.

"What? You don't find me a ten anymore?"

"Maybe a nine and a half," she got out.

"Just give me a few days, and I'll work myself back up."

He rested his hands on her hips and touched her lips gently with his. She leaned back against the wall. "Is that a promise?"

"That's a threat. I always make good on those." He pulled away and made a playful jab at her stomach. "How about some lunch?"

Ashton expelled a heavy sigh. "Seeing as how both stall and house are occupied, I suppose I have no choice but to satisfy my cravings with food."

"We'll satisfy all the other appetites later, my sweet!" He reached outside and presented her with a picnic hamper. "Voila! It just so happens that I already have our lunch packed. Sarah makes the best fried chicken in the county."

Ashton's nose wrinkled. "Don't you think you can create an atmosphere more romantic than a horse stall for our picnic?"

He offered her his arm. "This way, madame. Your table is waiting."

Cav spread a blanket beside the creek a while later. A weeping willow tree stood like an umbrella over the spot he had selected.

Ashton reclined on her elbows and gazed up at the low-hanging branches. "You've thought of everything, haven't you?"

"Naturally." He uncorked a bottle of wine. "Such ingenuity should not go unrewarded. It should be worth half a point, at least."

One leg dangled over the other. "I think I shall reserve judgment on that until later, if you don't mind." She sipped her wine slowly. "How did your meeting go with the electrical inspector?"

"No problems." He reached for a chicken leg. "Good thing, too. We're already booked solid through the holidays. I'd sure hate to delay our opening on account of poor construction."

Ashton leaned over the picnic basket. "I have it from a very reliable source that this venture of yours is going to be a tremendous success!" She clicked her plastic glass against his. "Watch out, Vail!"

"I'll drink to that!"

Seconds later, Cav took her glass from her hand and set it on the ground. His eyes devouring hers, he reached out to her. She didn't have to be asked twice. She was only too eager to oblige his every wish.

Laughing and nipping at each other like a pair of playful puppies, they tumbled back onto the blanket. His body welded to hers, and she soon forgot the chill in the early November air. Sparks crackled beneath their corduroys and wools. His kisses lit firecrackers inside her. Her senses went into orbit high above the treetops. Her skin tingled; she felt deliciously wanton. She was willing to risk even pneumonia if only he would make her his then and there.

"So tell me, how does one go about making reservations for *Wolf Lair's* grand opening?" she inquired after loud toots from the bulldozer operator had pried them apart.

Cav's face was sober. "Sorry, lady, but we're booked solid through New Year's." He spooned some potato salad onto his plate. "However, since you're on such good terms with the boss, I think you're eligible for a little preferential treatment."

Her hand ironed the wale of fabric ribbing the inside of

his leg. "Well, now, I certainly wouldn't want you to bend the rules on my account."

His gaze held hers. "I already have."

Ashton's heart braked, reversed, then skittered out of control. She had a feeling they were talking about two separate matters.

"What say I show you the hotel now?" asked Cav when the blanket was folded and the leftovers stowed in the hamper.

"I'd enjoy that." His earlier remark was still on her mind. How was she supposed to interpret that, she wondered, pulling herself up. Then again, she must be careful not to read anything into those three words that hadn't been intended.

"Hold this, will you?" He handed her the basket, then took off running. "Race you to the top."

"Look!" she exclaimed, pointing to the pump house.

Cav stopped. "What?"

She mouthed the word: "Bear."

"Bear?" laughed Cav. "Where?"

"Shh. Not so loud. You'll disturb him." Swinging the basket, she strode casually to where he stood. "See him?"

Cav shook his head and peered further into the woods.

She dropped the basket at his feet and bolted past. "SUCKER!" she called out over her shoulder.

Ashton sat Indian-style on a guanaco rug in front of the fire late that evening. Her back fit snugly against Cav's firm chest. Her head rested on his shoulder, and her hands lay flat against the muscles and sinews corralling her.

A half-moan, half-sigh of contentment escaped her lips. The atmosphere could not have been more ideal had it been created by a Hollywood designer for a prime-time seduction scene. Flames leapt high in the fireplace. The fawn-colored rug had fur so deep and thick that her bottom almost felt as if it were resting on air. What made the setting perfect, though, was the man behind her. His hundred and ninety pounds of carnal essence defined the meaning of the word virile. Just thinking of what she could look forward to when they ascended the stairs to his bedroom made her shake and tremble against him.

"You know something?" he whispered into her ear as the flames began to die. His voice was just as heady as the all-male scent that clung to him. "I have a notion to buy all of Bear Wallow just so I'll be in the position to have *Consolidated*'s chief geologist at my beck and call any time of the day or night."

Her breath flatly refused to be regulated in his presence. "What makes you think you have to wait until then?"

"I do have my reputation to consider."

Her palm pressed the inside of his thigh. "And I certainly wouldn't want you to compromise that."

"I don't suppose you could rearrange your schedule and stay through the weekend, could you?" he asked, his breath searing her neck.

"Well, I—I had planned on leaving Thursday," she finally managed.

"I know." He turned her around to face him. "But that's only two days away, and there's still a lot of territory in these mountains that you haven't even begun to cover." His mouth hooked in that sexy, devil-may-care grin she had come to adore.

"I wouldn't want to wear out my welcome. . . . or my host," she couldn't resist adding.

"Fat chance of that," he chuckled.

Laughing, she tried to wriggle out of his grasp, but he held her with arms of steel. She had to stay put. "All this time, I thought there wasn't a vain bone in your body," she teased.

"Just stating the facts, lady!" He swept aside her curly tresses and peppered tiny love bites all around her neck.

It was almost more than she could stand.

"Mmmm. Who am I to disagree?" Hot messages were flashing to every one of her erogenous zones.

He pulled her to him, and the soft twin rises beneath her sweater were crushed against him. He could feel their swollen tips through his shirt. "Just tell me what I have to do to convince you to devote more time to the study of North Carolina rocks, and I'll do it."

His caresses lifted her off the rug. "Well . . . since I do have a few sick days due me . . ."

"Yes?"

"And . . . since I haven't booked my return flight home . . ."

"As an added incentive," he murmured, "I'll fly you home myself." He punctuated his announcement with another nip on her neck. "It just so happens that the *Wolf Lair Corporation* has its own charter service."

"It does, does it?" Oh, how she was enjoying this!

He nodded. "That's not all. The pilot on the Bluefield run gives passengers all sorts of extra amenities."

She reveled in his nearness. "I had no idea your talents extended above the ground."

"There's a lot you don't know about me, sweetheart."

Ashton giggled. His Bogey imitation left much to be desired. "I can't wait to find out the rest!"

Cav sprang to his feet and pulled her up with him. "Let's go."

"Go where?" She grabbed hold of his arm.

"Down to what used to be the wine cellar." He took a bottle of champagne from the cooler and plucked two glasses from the rack above the bar. "Now it's my playroom."

"Sounds a little kinky to me."

He gave her a peck on the cheek. "So what? You're among friends." One arm draped around her shoulder, he led her out of the main room and through the kitchen.

"Too bad I forgot my leather whip and hip boots."

"We'll improvise." He opened the basement door and flipped on the stair lights. "Ladies first."

"Not this time." Her hand swept in front of her. "After you."

Cav led the way down. "Well, how do you like it?" he asked, reaching bottom.

"This is some set-up!" she exclaimed. "This place has more tone-up, trim-down, shape-up machines than a health and fitness studio." She hopped on the stationary bicycle and began pedaling with all her might. "I can feel the fat falling off my thighs already."

"Easy, kiddo. Don't wear yourself out so early."

She jumped off the bike and into his arms. "Got something better in mind, eh?"

"As a matter of fact, I do." Big, innocent eyes gleamed with devilment. "Undress, please."

She kicked her shoes across the room. "Whatever happened to subtle seduction?"

His face remained inscrutable. "Just do as you're told."

"My, my. Getting macho, aren't we?" She tugged her sweater over her head. "I would prefer doing this to music," she said, stepping out of her jeans in a striptease pantomime.

"Remind me to have a stereo system installed first thing tomorrow." His eyes raked her body with undisguised lust.

His hungry expression fueled the fire already burning in her. "First things first," she said, her voice low.

Ashton undressed him in her mind with each step she took in his direction. When she reached him, her fingers tore at his buttons. She couldn't wait to part the plaids and expose the field of curly tendrils carpeting his chest. Her chocolate-brown eyes shifted down to the contour of his hips a few seconds later. "I'm beginning to like this game more and more."

"I had a feeling you might." He slid her lace bikini down legs that ached to wind around him. Taking her by the hand, he led her into a smaller room adjoining the gym.

"I think I've died and gone to heaven!" Ashton exclaimed when she saw what the cedar walls enclosed. She swung her legs over the side of the hot tub and plunged feet first into the hot whirl. "Ahhh . . . you may never get rid of me now."

Cav dropped down beside her. "Smart girl. You're catching on fast."

She sunk deeper and deeper. "I'm so relaxed, I don't think I could budge from here if my life depended on it."

"There goes my fantasy," he sighed.

Ashton came alive quickly. Her hand dove under the water, and when it found its mark Cav's chest heaved and his breath came in ragged gasps. "I wouldn't jump to any conclusions if I were you," she told him.

She threw a leg over his hard thighs. "I have a feeling this just might be your lucky day." Anxious hips rolled towards him, and soft lips feasted on a kiss that was long and deep and wet.

She giggled as his mouth slid across her breasts, trying to gain possession of a pair of firm, ripe peaks that were slippery and glistening from the water. He lifted her hips higher, and then his head dove under the water. She felt his kisses on her stomach. His tongue showed no mercy. A storm erupted in the very core of her femininity. When he stopped to come up for air, she all but screamed.

Impatient hands grabbed hold of slippery buttocks.

Ashton was all too happy to grant him total access.

Emotions she had never felt before were surfacing now. Each breath she gasped was certain to be her last. She was about to be dragged from sanity by the very undertow she had helped to create.

Ashton lazed under a stack of quilts an hour later. Her body was still warm and moist from their lovemaking. "You know," she began, rolling over onto her side, "there's something about these North Carolina mountains that makes me voracious!"

Frowning, Cav reached for his robe. "You're a lot of trouble, woman."

Her fingers skimmed his chest. "Ah, but worth it."

"Alright," he grumbled. "I'll go down and whip up some omelets for supper. But only because you're company," he added, giving her toes a tweak.

Ashton threw back the covers and patted the big, empty space he had just vacated, grinning at him. "Cav, I said nothing about food."

Chapter Eight

Ashton led Calandre down the side of Wolf Mountain. Weighting down the mare's saddlebags were samples from every outcropping on Bear Wallow's southwest slope.

Every rock had been labeled and categorized according to the location where it had been found. Her suspicions of the past few days had proven correct. Mining the gallium on Bear Wallow would not be cost efficient. The heaviest concentration of the metal was limited to a section where restrictions imposed by nature made mining it next to impossible. There was no doubt in her mind. *Consolidated* had no choice but to locate another source of gallium elsewhere.

Ashton wasn't quite sure if she should be pleased or disappointed by her findings. From a strictly nonprofessional view, it would be a shame to destroy such beauty. On the other hand, common sense told her that if Bear Wallow did not provide *Consolidated* and other companies with the gallium they needed, some other mountain would. Sometimes she felt like such a hypocrite. She had chosen geology as her field of study because she appreciated the splendor of the outdoors. What had begun as a childhood fascination more often than not resulted in the demise of the very land she loved. More than once she had asked herself whether or not the fat paycheck she drew each month was worth compromising her values.

Ashton stopped at the spot where she and Cav had

picnicked. Looping Calandre's reins over a tree branch, she sat down beside the creek to catch her second wind before tackling the last leg of her journey.

Zebo dropped a stick at her feet.

She threw it out for him to retrieve. "Good boy," she praised, patting the dog on the head when he returned it.

Ashton pulled back her arm a second time. The shuffling of dry leaves somewhere close to her made her drop her arm back down to her side.

Zebo rumbled a low growl.

She grabbed him by his collar. "Easy, boy. Nothing to worry about."

She knew her words of assurance had been directed to herself more than to the dog. A sneaking suspicion that she was not the only trespasser on Bear Wallow had gnawed at her all day long. She reminded herself that any person who tried to tangle with her would have his hands full. Not only had Zebo been trained to attack on command, she, herself, had completed a self-defense class with honors last spring.

Ashton stood up. She listened and watched and waited. The woods across the creek were quiet—too quiet, as far as she was concerned.

A flash of red in the bushes behind the pump house caught her eye.

"Who's there?" she demanded.

Zebo broke free of her hold. He charged across the creek, snarling and churning up the water.

"Zebo. Here, boy. Zebo," she called after him.

The shepherd bolted into the bushes and disappeared into the thicket.

Ashton called his name repeatedly. All she could hear was him barking as he bounded through the brush.

There was a single blast from a rifle. To her horror, Ashton heard Zebo yelping in pain, and then heavy footsteps thumping the ground sounded one right after the other.

Calandre whinnied, frightened, but Ashton ignored her, and tore across the creek in the direction of the noises.

Zebo was lying beside the pump house. The fur around his neck was matted with blood. She dropped to her knees beside him and felt for a pulse. The beat was definite.

She gently lowered his head back to the ground. "Hang on, fellow. I'll be right back. Just hang on."

She sprinted back to Calandre, stripped the heavy packs from the mare's back and leaped into the saddle, urging the horse to a gallop. As the *Wolf Lair* construction site came into view, she began yelling for Cav at the top of her lungs. The silver pickup was nowhere around. Neither was Bud's jeep. She called out to Hank as his Blazer drove past. The bulldozer operator waved and grinned and continued down the road. She jumped off the horse and ran on toward the trailer in hopes that one of the men would be working overtime. Her stride shortened into a jog. The cream-colored Mercedes was parked beside the office. Standing on the porch with cigarette in hand was Hampton Breyer.

"Where's Cav?" she shouted at the end of the road.

Breyer pointed to his ear and walked down the drive to meet her. "I'm sorry. What did you say?" His sphinxlike countenance cracked when he had come several steps closer. "Good God! Are you alright? What happened?" he questioned, eyeing the splatters of blood on her jacket.

"It's Zebo," she gasped between breaths. "He's been shot. Have you seen Cav?"

Breyer grabbed hold of her arm. "Where?"

She pointed in the direction of the pump house. "Over there. In the bushes across the creek."

Breyer flipped his cigarette onto the gravel and grabbed hold of her arm. "Come on."

Ashton jerked free. "Where are you taking me?"

Breyer looked at her like she was mad. "To get Zebo and take him to the vet. Do you want to go with me or not?"

She called to a man who had just emerged from the toolshed to take care of Calandre, then mutely followed Breyer out to his car, feeling like a fool for even checking his shoes for mud.

Wheeling his Mercedes around like it was a jeep, Breyer

spun across the field. Gullies and ridges tore at the car's underside. Arriving at the pump house, he slung the gear into park and bolted out of the car and across the creek.

She caught up just as he whipped off his blazer and wrapped it around the dog.

"Don't worry, pal, you'll be fine," she heard him tell Zebo in a tone that was much kinder than the one he used to address humans.

"You drive!" he shouted after loading the dog into the back seat. "He's liable to get pretty testy if the pain gets worse." With that, he slid in beside Zebo.

With Breyer urging her to drive faster and faster, she careened around one sharp curve after another. All the way down the mountain, she could hear him mumbling words of reassurance to the dog.

"Hang left at the depot," he instructed as they entered town from the west. "Hold on, fellow. Just a little longer."

Ashton bumped across the railroad track at a speed triple that of the posted limit. "How's he doing?"

"He's lost a lot of blood," came the grave reply from the back.

"Think he'll make it?"

"I don't know," he mumbled. "Pull in here!" he exclaimed, pointing to a cedar-shingled building.

She swerved into a gravel lot. The car spun around several times before coming to a stop. Before she had time to cut the engine, Breyer had Zebo in his arms.

"Get Dr. Marshall," he yelled to the kennel man. "Now!" he shouted impatiently. "Not next week."

A woman with a gray ponytail swung open the screen door. "Isn't that Cav Cavanaugh's dog?"

Ashton nodded. "He's been shot. It looks awfully bad."

"Bring him through," she told Breyer, leading the way. She pointed to the examining table. "Strap him down." Her frown didn't leave her face the entire time she examined him. After giving Zebo an injection, she explained that the bullet was lodged in his neck. "All I can do is operate," she concluded. "Chances are he might not even make it then.

He's already lost a lot of blood." She looked from Breyer to Ashton and back to Breyer. "Okay, you two. Out! I can take it from here."

"I'll call the bank and see if Cav's still there," Ashton told Breyer as they made their way back to the waiting room. She joined him a few minutes later with news that she had caught Cav at the bank in time.

Ashton paced the floor and waited for Cav to get there. Breyer stood against the wall. His head was laid back on the paneling. He offered her a cigarette. She shook her head. His hand had a slight quiver to it when he lit one for himself.

Breyer drew hard on his cigarette. Smoke rolling from the corners of his mouth, he cursed hunters who held no respect for land that was posted as private. "Any one of them who can't tell a deer from a dog should be shot with his own rifle."

Ashton stopped pacing and faced him squarely. "I don't believe any mistake was made," she announced quietly.

He eyed her curiously. "Do you mean to say—"

She cut him off. "What I mean to say is that the person who shot Zebo knew damn well he was shooting at a dog."

"What makes you think that?"

Her hands burrowed in her pockets. "It's just a feeling. I can't put it into words."

Breyer stepped closer. "Surely your suspicions must have a basis." He stubbed out his cigarette in an ashtray.

"All day long," she began, frowning, "I've had the feeling that someone was following me and Zebo." She took a deep breath and leveled her eyes to his. "All day long, I've had the feeling that someone was stalking us."

Breyer took another cigarette from his gold case. "Our imaginations can play funny tricks on us, Miss Paro." He examined the filter before sticking it into his mouth. "We tend to let our minds get the best of us when we're alone or when we're in an unfamiliar environment."

"I'm aware of that, Mr. Breyer." Her eyes locked with his. "But I hardly think it was my imagination that spooked the horse I was riding and nearly sent us nose-diving into Indian Falls day before yesterday."

"Good God!" He sat down in one of the cane-backed chairs. "This happened Tuesday, you say?"

She nodded. "I took Calandre on a trail ride shortly after you and your sister left."

"What exactly happened?"

Ashton sat down beside him. For the first time since meeting him, she did not feel as if she were on the defensive. "I stopped to take a picture of the falls, and someone fired a couple of shots in our direction. Calandre started bucking and rearing. We were lucky we didn't plunge down the ravine."

Breyer shook his head. "I can't understand it. Nobody from around here hunts on Bear Wallow. They all know better."

"At first I thought I just happened to be in the wrong place at the wrong time. But now . . ." she hesitated.

"Now?"

She held his stare. "Now I'm not sure. Too many things have happened this week." For a moment, she thought he was going to give her hand a pat. Instead, his own hand drew back and rested on his knee.

"If that's the case, Miss Paro, you're lucky that you weren't the one who caught the bullet."

His words hit home. "Yes, I know that."

Cav burst through the door a few minutes later. "What happened? Are you alright? Where's Zebo?"

Ashton met him halfway across the room. "I'm so sorry this happened. I should have never taken Zebo out with me this morning."

Cav slipped his arm around her waist. "It wasn't your fault, honey. Even had I been with the two of you, chances are the same thing would still have happened."

Breyer walked towards them.

"Had it not been for Mr. Breyer," began Ashton, seeing his questioning look, "Zebo wouldn't have made it this far.

He drove over to the creek to get him, then brought us into town."

Cav held out his hand. "Thanks, Hamp. I really appreciate it."

Ashton wondered how her initial impression of Breyer could have been so far off base. "That goes for me, too. I don't believe I've even thanked you yet."

Their words of gratitude seemed to make Breyer uncomfortable. "Please, you don't have to thank me. I'm just glad I happened along when I did."

Ashton was certain she saw cracks in the hard, sculpted lines cornering his mouth. "So am I," she said quietly. "So am I."

Ashton couldn't help but feel a little guilty at having formed such an instant dislike for him on Monday. Once he thawed, he really was quite likeable. There was a lot to be said for someone who showed such kindness to a helpless animal, she reminded herself.

"I'm sure Zebo will be just fine," he told Cav. "You won't find a better vet than Eva Marshall anywhere." He checked his watch. "Since everything seems to be under control here, I'll be on my way. Let me know how things turn out, will you?"

Ashton picked up the wool bundle from the floor. "Don't worry about this. I'll have it cleaned and delivered to your office first thing tomorrow."

Breyer took his blazer from her. "No need to bother. Really. I'll drop it off on my way home." He turned back midway to the door. "Incidentally, Cav, I brought those preliminary survey reports by your office. I couldn't find Bud around, so I left them on your desk."

Ashton sensed his words were directed more to her than to Cav. Breyer didn't need ESP to know that she had been suspicious of his presence at the trailer at that exact moment.

Cav snapped his fingers. "That's right. I was supposed to meet with you. I apologize. I got tied up at the bank and forgot all about it."

Breyer waved aside his apologies. "That's perfectly alright. I understand how bankers are. Once they get you in their office, they won't let go." He took out his gold cigarette case, then slipped it back down into his pants pocket. "One more thing. The surveyor needs the aerial shots by Monday. Think you can have them for him by then?"

Cav nodded. "I've been meaning to do that all week and just haven't gotten around to it." He gave Ashton's arm a squeeze. "We'll do that first thing tomorrow. You're welcome to go up with us, if you'd like," he told Breyer.

Laughing, Breyer shook his head. "Anything smaller than a 727 gives me claustrophobia. Give me a call, though, before you leave. I might have changed my mind by then."

"What's this 'we' business?" asked Ashton after the Mercedes had rolled out of the lot.

Cav twisted her arm behind her. "Didn't I tell you that you've been appointed official photographer of *Wolf Lair Corporation?*"

"Sorry to disappoint you," she said, using one of the moves she had been taught in her self-defense class to free herself, "but if you think I'm going to hang out of a plane taking pictures for a surveyor, you've got a few screws loose." She gave him a mischievous smile. "However, I will be more than happy to man the controls while you dangle out at five thousand feet. That is, unless you object to having a woman in the cockpit," she couldn't resist adding.

Cav sidled closer. "I reckon that's as good a place as any for them."

Dr. Marshall appeared half an hour later wearing a smile that assured them Zebo had pulled through. "I would like to keep him with me through the weekend. Not that I'm expecting any complications, mind you, but you never know when an infection might set in." She handed a bullet to Cav. "This missed his main artery by only a fraction of an inch."

Cav examined it, then passed it on to Ashton. "It looks

like a slug from a thirty-thirty. That's what they use around here to hunt deer." He shook his head angrily. "You'd think those hunters could tell the difference between a deer and a dog, wouldn't you?"

"Some of these fellows are so anxious to bag a big buck, they'll shoot at anything that moves." She turned to Ashton and held out her hand. "I don't believe we've been introduced. I'm Eva Marshall."

Ashton returned her smile and grip when she told the vet her name.

The vet's eyes narrowed. "Paro? You're not from around here, are you?"

Ashton shook her head. "My home's in West Virginia."

"I didn't think Paro was a name common to these parts." She slipped out of her surgical jacket. "No point in you folks hanging around here. Run along home now. Zebo's out of the woods. He's going to be alright. I promise."

Chapter Nine

Ashton and Cav sat blanketed in front of the fire a few hours later. A bottle of Chianti and a pizza take-out box were positioned between them.

Cav rested his hand on Ashton's arm. "What's wrong?" he asked quietly.

She lifted his hand and brushed it with her lips. "What makes you think anything's wrong?"

"For starters, ever since we got home I've been delivering one monologue after another," he answered quickly.

"But I've been listening."

He smiled. "And nodding politely from time to time. I'm on to you." He took the slice of pizza from her hand and dropped it back down into the box. "What really gave you away, though, is that you've been nibbling on that same spot for half an hour now."

"You don't miss much, do you?"

Cav moved the box to the hearth and scooted closer. "Come on. You have before you a jug of fine vino, a meal fit for the galloping gourmet, and an admirer who thinks you're the next best thing to peanut butter pie. So, why the long face?" He tilted her chin up so that she faced him. "Hey, you're not still blaming yourself for Zebo's accident, are you?"

"It wasn't an accident, Cav." Her voice was firm and certain.

His smile vanished. "What makes you say that?"

Ashton knew she just couldn't keep her suspicions to herself another minute. She had to reveal them to Cav. If he thought she was crazy, fine! "In the first place, Zebo tore across that creek barking so loudly he could have been heard all the way to Rosman." She looked straight at him. "Secondly, doesn't it strike you odd that a hunter wouldn't come to check out his kill? For all he knew, he could have hit a big buck."

Cav scratched his chin. "I see your point. If he didn't know he was shooting at a dog, why didn't he come see what he had shot?" He reached for her hand. "And if he did know he was shooting at a dog, why did he go ahead and shoot?"

"Exactly." She leaned back against the couch. "Whoever pulled that trigger knew good and well they were shooting at a dog. The way I was yelling for Zebo to come back, they would have had to be deaf not to have known."

His fingers tightened around hers. "I don't guess you think what happened to you and Calandre up at Indian Falls was an accident either, do you?"

"No, I don't," she answered without hesitation. "Those shots were meant to spook me and her."

Cav let out a long, hard breath. "Do you have any idea why someone would be harassing you?"

"I'm not quite sure. Not yet." Her lips pursed in meditation. "But I'll tell you this much. I'm getting pretty fed up with all these occurrences that can't be explained. First, my room was turned upside down. The next day, someone was taking pot shots at me and the horse. Now, two days later, this has happened to Zebo."

Ashton stretched out flat on the rug. Her eyes focused on the rafters above. "If I were a neurotic female, I might consider the possibility that I had a persecution complex, but since I'm not . . ." Her voice trailed away.

"But since you're not what?" urged Cav, reclining beside her.

Her head found its way to his chest. "Since I don't have

neurotic tendencies, I'm inclined to believe that someone is trying to get a message across to me."

Cav's jaw hardened. "What kind of message?"

"Leave—or else," she answered simply.

"Why you?"

Ashton stared off into space. "I have no idea. If I did, I'd be doing something about it." Her fist slammed against the floor. "It's like one giant jigsaw puzzle. All the pieces are lined up right in front of me, but I can't get any of them to fit together."

Cav said nothing.

"I'm not paranoid, you know," she told him a few minutes later.

His face grayed. "I know you're not, babe. I agree with you. There have been too many unexplained happenings lately for my liking, too."

"Maybe there's something to Molly's theory about a kook being on the loose around here," she considered aloud.

Cav disagreed. "You yourself know that a stranger can't go unnoticed around here for one minute."

"I'd hate to think someone I know has been responsible for all these 'accidents'," she said shivering.

"So would I, sweetheart, but right now everyone's suspect." He tucked the afghan closer around her chin. "Tell you what. Let's make a list of everyone you've met in Fox Run and work from there."

"Then you think the person responsible is someone I know?"

Cav shook his head. "I didn't say that. All I'm suggesting is that we need to consider all possibilities."

"You're right," she sighed. "Alright, I'll start from the time I arrived in town." A smile replaced her dour expression. "Numero Uno—Cav Cavanaugh."

"I'm honored you hold me in such high esteem, but I hardly think I can be considered your prime suspect." He hugged her close. "You mustn't forget that had I wanted to do you harm, I've had more than enough opportunities."

Last night's embers began smouldering inside her. "Business first," she reminded him, playfully pushing him away.

"You're right. Number two?"

She thought for a moment. "Number two would be Pop down at the filling station. He did act very peculiar, you know."

"That's Pop for you, but he's harmless. Next?"

Ashton closed her eyes and tried to retrace her moves from the minute she entered Fox Run. "The secretary in the courthouse. What was her name? Lou Ann?"

"Beth Ann," he corrected. "Now that's a very distinct possibility."

Her nose wrinkled. "How so?"

Cav's eyes were wide with innocence. "After all, I did take you to lunch."

She punched him in the stomach. "I shall ignore that remark, thank you."

His hand crept along the soft inside of her thighs, raising goosebumps on her flesh. "Just trying to cover all the angles."

"Let's leave some of the angles for later, shall we?" She deposited his hand back onto his stomach. "Let's see now, from the courthouse I went to Varner's. There I met Myra, Mr. Breyer, and a half-dozen no-names who must have bruised ribs from poking each other in the sides when we walked in."

Cav sat up. "Did you ever make any sense out of Myra's warning?"

Ashton frowned. "No, I didn't. She wasn't too anxious to clarify matters for me, either."

"Did you mention anything about it to Molly?" he asked.

She nodded. "Molly just said that Breyer had a reputation of being somewhat of a lady's man and that Myra was just giving me advance notice."

Cav chuckled.

"What's so funny?"

"If anybody should know town scuttlebutt, it'd be Molly," he finally answered. "But I swear, I can't picture Hamp as a Don Juan."

She shrugged her shoulders. "That's what she said. Has he ever been married?" she asked a moment later.

Cav nodded. "From what I hear, he was married to some judge's daughter for about fifteen years. Then, she just up and left him one day. He never remarried."

"Maybe that's why he's so hard to get to know," she said. "He could have been hurt very badly at one time."

"Could be."

"Alright," she continued with a sigh. "After lunch, I met Fred Isaacs, then Molly, and Sergeant Kelly later on."

"Since then?" probed Cav.

She thought for a moment. "Let me see. Bud . . . Judith . . . Sarah . . . the two men who took my car back to Asheville—"

"—Hank and Roy—"

"That's right. Hank and Roy." Her index finger tapped at her chin. "Dr. Marshall . . . I guess that's it." She threw up her hands in despair. "You know, wracking our brains for names is getting us nowhere fast. Not one of the people mentioned has any reason to want to harm me or get me out of town."

Frowning, Cav poured them another glass of Chianti. "As long as we're grabbing at loose ends, perhaps we shouldn't totally rule out the possibility that one of *Consolidated*'s competitors is somehow involved in all this."

She sipped her wine slowly. "No, I don't think so," she disagreed. "First of all, anyone new in town would stand out like a sore thumb. Look at me! Secondly, scare tactics just isn't their style. Extortion, bribery, blackmail, maybe, but not kid stuff."

"I hardly think any of this can be interpreted as kid's stuff," he reminded her.

"You're right," she swallowed hard. "I shouldn't be so flip about it. I could easily have been killed when Calandre reared." The import of what she had said hit home immediately. She really could have been killed!

What if the person standing behind the gun had pulled the trigger knowing full well the horse was only a few steps away from the ledge? Icy fingers stabbed her spine. Suppose the shots had been intended for her but hit Zebo instead?

Suddenly, she was afraid—very afraid. If someone were after her, then what next? What else had been planned for her? Someone had to be stalking her, she decided. Absently she found the gold rosebud hidden in the folds of her sweater and clinched it tightly. Otherwise, how would he have known her every move? He was the hunter. She was the prey. Undoubtedly, he was waiting until his prey was most vulnerable before closing in again.

She shivered and Cav drew her into his arms, rubbing her back to warm her, mussing her hair with tender kisses on the top of her head. Sighing, Ashton gave herself up to his care. The anger at her unknown assailant remained— but, for the moment, she was content to be cuddled. Tomorrow she would be ready to fight back . . . right now, she just wanted to be loved.

Chapter Ten

Aѕнтон walked through the pre-flight inspection of Cav's CESSNA 310 with an alert eye. "She's in fine shape," she told Cav after completing the examination.

"Should be. I had her overhauled back in the summer." He gave her a boost onto the wing. "She's not all that's in good shape around here," he said, patting Ashton's backside as she swung herself into the cockpit.

Ashton buckled herself into the pilot's seat. "Just think what great condition I'll be in after my twelve-hundred-mile overhaul."

"I can't wait!" He slammed the door, strapped the seat belt around himself, then gave Ashton a salute. "First officer Cavanaugh reporting for duty sir . . . uh . . . m'am."

"Good help sure is hard to find these days." She gave him the once-over. "I guess you'll have to do."

Ashton flipped on the master switch and checked the carburetor heat and oil mixture before giving the primer pump a few strokes. After checking the propeller area and calling out "Clear," she switched on the left engine, then the right. While the engines were revving up, she gave the controls another quick check.

Cav gave her a thumbs-up sign.

She pushed the throttle full forward.

The CESSNA rolled down the runway, gathering speed en route.

"Nice job," applauded Cav when the plane had broken ground.

"Did you expect less?" she asked as they began their climb.

"Not from you." He fitted the zoom lens onto the camera. "Tell me. Is there anything you can't do?"

Ashton retracted the landing gear. "Plenty, but I shan't bore you with the details now."

"No doubt your attributes far outweigh any minor deficiencies." Cav focused the camera on her. "Smile." He snapped a half-dozen pictures in sequence.

"You never did tell me how you got interested in flying," he reminded her a few minutes later.

Her eyes stayed glued to the panel. "I had a great teacher."

"Who was that?"

"My dad," she answered. "He used to fly commercially for *Southeast Air,* and before that he was a Navy fighter pilot."

Cav leaned back in his seat. "I see. You've got it in your blood, huh?"

She leveled the plane off at four thousand feet. "Something like that," she finally replied.

"You truly are one amazing female." Cav leaned across and gave her a peck on the cheek. "Ready for your initiation into the mile high club?"

Ashton flashed him a wide grin. "You just stick to your picture-taking, please."

She sat back and enjoyed the spectacular view unfolding around them. Shafts of gold showering through the sky bathed the land below in a kind of spiritual aura. The perfect shadow the CESSNA cast on the bunched treetops made it seem as though a giant streamlined bird were soaring above in flight.

Ashton could not help but smile. How she loved being at the controls! Everything about flying exhilarated her. She caught a glimpse of Cav out of the corner of her eye. It was apparent by his expression that he had as much confidence in her skill as a pilot as she. The man truly was remarkable!

"Look, down there is *Wolf Lair*," she pointed out a short while later. "I'll get down a little closer so you can get some good shots of the construction."

Cav began clicking shots. "Just leave the treetops."

"You just worry about that fancy piece of equipment of yours," she told him, buzzing the site. "Let me worry about the rest."

"That should do it," he told her after taking pictures of his project from all angles.

Nodding, she banked the plane to the left and headed toward the eastern slope of Bear Wallow.

"How's that?" she asked as they made the fourth sweep of the area he needed to photograph for the surveyor.

"Perfecto! Any closer and I could reach out and pick you a daisy. Once more should do it." His hand shimmied up her leg. "Then we can get on with your initiation."

She brushed away his hand. "You know, for a co-pilot, you sure do take a lot of liberties with the boss!"

With that, she banked the plane slowly for one more time around.

Halfway into the turn, the plane began sputtering.

Frowning, she looked out the window. Shocked, she saw that sparks were shooting out from the left engine.

"What do you think? Water in the fuel line?" queried Cav, peering over her shoulder.

"No way! I drained that first thing." Her eyes shot down to the control panel. "Pressure's dropping fast." Her gaze cut back outside. Oil was splattering onto the wing.

"Altitude dropping," he informed her, his eyes glued to the gauges.

"We're losing oil, too," she added.

"You know what to do, babe," he said encouragingly. "I've got all the confidence in the world in you."

Ashton nodded. No reason to panic, she told herself. She knew exactly what to do. More than once her dad had stalled an engine in flight in order to prepare her for an emergency such as the one confronting her now. This time's no different, she tried to convince herself.

"Here goes." Hand on throttle, she cut power on the left engine and increased on the right at the same time.

"Good job," complimented Cav, his voice still steady. "You got it now!"

Ashton took a deep breath. She wished he were right, but she knew better. The worst was yet to come. Without full power, the plane would lose both speed and altitude at an increasing rate.

She gripped the wheel tighter. Holding the plane steady was next to impossible. Still, the shaking feeling in the stick was not a new experience. Thank God, she had been prepared for every emergency possible. So many times her dad had insisted on playing a game of pretend with her at the controls. What would you do if. . . . She only hoped she would be able to tell him that she had learned those lessons well.

"Nice going," said Cav. "You're doing just fine."

Ashton gave a weak nod. If he doubted her ability, he certainly wasn't showing it! For that, she was relieved. Now, if she could only get them down in one piece.

"Altitude?" she asked a few moments later.

"Three thousand . . . and dropping."

She quickly checked the instrument readings, then computed her rate of descent. If she could control the descent to two hundred feet per minute, they stood a chance. An excellent chance, in fact.

Confident, she turned the plane back toward the airfield. Neither of them dared to speak until the runway was in sight. She checked the panel a final time. "Altitude twelve hundred feet." She'd be cutting it close!

"You got all the time in the world, hon," Cav told her soothingly. "You're doing great."

"Keep your fingers crossed." She lowered the landing gear. "Wing flap down. . . . Throttle retracted." With one more deep breath and a pep talk to herself, she banked left and headed in for the final approach.

The end of the runway came up to meet them.

"So far so good," she said, half to herself, scarcely breathing.

Cav let out a cheer. "Right on the money!"

Catching a good breath at last, Ashton raised the nose. The sound of wheels skidding along the strip was music to her ears. She slumped against the seat. At four thousand feet, she couldn't afford to be afraid. Now, the real panic was about to set it. She could feel it skittering through her veins in a delayed reaction.

Cav combed his fingers through her curls. "You sure earned your wings today, pretty lady."

She opened her mouth to speak, but the witty comeback she had intended to deliver stuck in her throat. She managed a weak nod instead and taxied down the runway in silence.

She couldn't get her feet planted firmly on the ground fast enough to suit her. Once there, she was certain her legs were about to come flying out from under her.

"I feel like I'm leading a cursed existence," she told Cav, steadying herself against his sturdy frame. "You know you might be safer if I walk a few paces behind you."

Strong fingers wove themselves tightly around her waist. "No way. You're not getting off that easy," he told her. "We're in this together. You just remember that!"

His smile was strained. She could sense it; she didn't need to ask him why. Ashton knew their thoughts were on the same wavelength and had been ever since four thousand feet. Neither had been able to ask the question aloud. Had the CESSNA been sabotaged? Even the question chilled her. If her suspicions were right, then the person responsible was getting down to business in a hurry. There may have been some doubt before, but not now. Someone was definitely out to get her.

Ashton pulled herself up onto the port wing. She knew what she would discover without taking the cowling from the engine. A single oil line would be loosened just enough so that the engine's vibrations would take care of the rest.

Cav took a look inside. "Something like that would never have been detected in a routine pre-flight exam." He shook his head thoughtfully. "Somebody sure knew what he was up to."

"No doubt about that," she agreed.

After refitting the cowling, she jumped down. Her hands dug deep into the pockets of her sheepskin jacket. "Thank God it was only one engine. At least we were able to limp in. I hate to think what would have happened if . . ."

She couldn't continue. Her body went numb beneath the layers of wool. With both engines down, the plane would have crashed into the side of the mountain, and nothing she might have done could have prevented it. They would have been goners for sure. One more small-plane crack-up would have most likely been chalked up to pilot error.

Why? Who? The same two questions kept echoing in her head. Three attempts had been made on her life, and still she knew no more then than she had known two days ago. How much time did she have left to find out, she wondered dismally. One thing was certain. She had to get him before he got her!

"No suspects, no motives. Worst still, no clues!" she exclaimed inside the truck. "Someone wants me dead, and I don't have the slightest idea why. For that matter, I don't even know where to look for the answers." She expelled a troubled sigh. "The hell of it is, I'm not sure I'd even know the right questions to ask if I did!"

The truck wheeled out of the lot slinging gravel behind it.

"Yeah, I know what you mean," agreed Cav, his words heavy. "I know what you mean."

Ashton sank deeper into the leather seat. "So who knew we were going up to take pictures today?"

"Just about everybody at the project, and you know how easily word could have gotten around from there." He reached for her hand and clasped it tight. "We're not doing very well at narrowing down the list of potential suspects, are we, babe?"

The sound of his voice and the feel of his flesh on hers filled her with renewed hope. "Not yet, but we will." We have to, she added silently. If not . . . well, if not, the future did not look all that promising.

Cav slowed in front of the courthouse. "What would you think of reporting to Sergeant Kelly all that's happened since we last saw him?" he suggested.

Ashton waved him on. "You know as well as I that he'll just tell you that's the chance you take when a woman is at the controls of a plane." She tugged at her gold rosebud. "As for the other incidences, he'll just say that Calandre was spooked by a ricochet, and Zebo was shot by a poacher who ran away because he thought he was about to get caught."

"You've made your point," he admitted hesitantly. "But tell me, if you don't want to involve the police, what exactly do you intend to do?"

"I intend to get to the bottom of this myself!" she answered, her words crisp and succinct. "I'm tired of being the mouse in this cat and mouse game. From now on, I'm going to be the cat. I'll get that bastard." She dropped her necklace back under her sweater. "You just wait. I'll fix him good."

Cav grinned. "All by yourself, no doubt." He pulled her across the seat. "Just in case you're the least bit interested, you're not in this alone, you know."

The tension drained from her body. His nearness was so soothing. "You might just regret that gallant gesture."

He shook his head. "Not on your life."

She made a sour face. "Poor choice of words."

A while later, Ashton laid her head on his shoulder, then jerked it up in the same instant. "Wait a minute. I think I may have just hit on something. Maybe even a motive," she exclaimed excitedly.

Cav's enthusiasm matched her own. "Let's hear it."

She turned sideways to face him. "Keep an open mind now, because this might sound a little crazy."

"Go on."

"Well," she began eagerly. "Remember what Myra said about me being the spitting image of a girl who used to live in Fox Run?"

He nodded.

"And before that, Pop had been so certain that I was from these parts." She paused and took a deep breath. "Suppose the fruitcake we're dealing with came to the same conclusion?"

"Mistaken identity?" he asked.

Ashton nodded. "Maybe it's this other woman he's out to get. That's the only explanation that sounds the least bit feasible. I just have the misfortune of resembling her to a T." As an afterthought, she asked, "I wonder what this mystery woman might have done to incur so much hatred. It must have been pretty bad to make someone want to kill for it. Well, what do you think?" she asked, quickly returning to the matter at hand before her imagination steamed on at full speed.

"I don't think it sounds crazy at all," Cav said after a while. "As a matter of fact, I think you may just be right." His tone was grave. "Now all we have to do is convince that maniac that he's after the wrong woman, before . . ."

He didn't have to complete the sentence. She knew only too well what he was thinking.

Chapter Eleven

"COULD it be possible that you have relatives in western North Carolina?"

Cav's query came as no surprise. She had posed the same question to herself most of the way through lunch. "It is possible I have relatives somewhere in the state," replied Ashton thoughtfully, "but I couldn't pinpoint the exact location." She pushed back her bowl of pintos and folded her arms across the table. "You see, odds are that I was born in North Carolina. Where, I don't know."

Cav frowned. "I'm not sure I understand."

"Neither do I. Not really." Smiling, she explained. "The Paros aren't my biological parents. They adopted me from the children's home in Raleigh. I was only five at the time. They were stationed in Wilmington, and when Dad retired from the Navy, we moved to West Virginia."

Cav blew on a spoonful of beans. "So what about your natural parents?"

"I know nothing about them. Don't really care to, to be honest with you." The rosebud slid from one side of the chain to the other. "A highway patrolman found me wandering down the side of the road all by myself. My clothes were torn and I had cuts and bruises all over me, so the police naturally assumed I had been abused and abandoned." She absently fingered the tiny diamond in the center of the gold rose. "No one reported me missing, and no one ever came to claim me. I was only in the children's

home for a month or so before the Paros took me. I had
lived with them for several weeks before I even told them
my given name. The only other thing I ever told them
about myself was that I had a cat named Buster. That's
all," she said, a distant look on her face. "Nothing else. I
don't know if I couldn't remember any other details, or if I
just chose not to."

"I'm sorry," said Cav softly, taking her hand.

"Don't be," she insisted. "Really. I couldn't have had
better folks had I picked them myself. Genes and chromo-
somes mean nothing, you know. A kid needs lots of love,
and believe me, I got more than my share from those two!"
She let the pendant drop back down onto the green and
pink argyle. "So getting back to your question, yes, I could
have relatives in this state, or in any other for that matter,
and never know it."

His brow arched. She knew what he was thinking. The
same thing was on her mind, too.

"Even in Fox Run?" he asked finally.

"Could be. Could very well be," she echoed softly.

Ashton glanced at the clock a few minutes later. "Hey,
it's nearly one," she announced, rising from the table. "If
the meeting with your CPA is still on, you'd better get
going."

"You're right. His time is my money." Cav pulled on his
jacket. "So what's on your agenda for the rest of the afternoon?"

She helped him fasten the snaps. "I need to finish typing
up the results of the study and get it in the mail. Call the
office, check with Sid, maybe run a few errands in town,"
she added after a pause.

"I'm not so sure I like the idea of you going into Fox Run
alone," frowned Cav. "I'd sure feel a lot better if you'd let
me send Hank or Roy with you."

"What for? To help me carry my packages?" She hurried
him out of the kitchen. "I'm a big girl. Remember? I can
take care of myself."

"Just make sure you—"

"I know," she interrupted. "Lock all doors, don't talk to strange men, and stay away from airplanes." She stood on tiptoes to kiss his check. "Now, get out of here."

"Don't rush me!" Cav hooked his fingers into her belt and yanked her against him. "If Sid objects too strongly about you staying on a few days, I'll see what I can do about putting you on *Wolf Lair*'s payroll."

"Mmm." She whispered huskily, "I'll keep that in mind."

Being on *Wolf Lair*'s payroll would definitely have its advantages, she decided, reveling in a kiss that was long and hard and deep. The fringe benefits alone would make it most worthwhile.

"Keys are in the pickup," he said when they finally managed to pry themselves apart. "You may need to pull into the shed and have it filled up." One more quick kiss, and he was on his way. "Keep the home fires burning," he called over his shoulder.

Ashton watched as his company car disappeared around the bend in a cloud of dust. His parting words rang in her ears. Keep the home fires burning!

She hugged her arms tight around her waist. Yes sireee, that definitely had a cozy sound to it!

She walked out of the post office later that afternoon humming happily to herself. Her report had been weighed, stamped and sent on its way. *Consolidated* should have it first thing Monday morning. When she had called Sid after lunch, he had been disappointed in the findings, but at least he had agreed that a few days R-and-R was due her. She didn't have to be back at work until Wednesday morning. Five whole days. Those extra hours with Cav would just make leaving him all the more difficult, she decided as she hopped into the pickup. Now that she had found the man of every woman's dreams, she couldn't stand the thought of letting him out of her sight, even for a minute. Cav had promised to fly up to visit a couple of times a month, and she was certain he would keep his word. Still, a weekend romance just wouldn't be the same. They both knew it, even though neither would admit to it. If only there had been a substantial deposit of gallium on *Bear Wallow,* she wished. That way, she could have worked it so at least one month out of four could be spent in Fox Run. If only . . .

Her mouth went dry. If only she could find out who was responsible for those "accidents" before that creep spoiled what time she had left with Cav.

Keeping one eye on the rearview mirror, Ashton made her way through Fox Run driving down one street and up the next. If someone were following her, she was positive the indirect routing would have given him away at once. No suspicious-looking vehicles were in sight fifteen minutes later when she turned onto Highway 64 and headed down to the gas station.

She turned into the gas station and pulled up alongside the full-service pump. Watching from the rearview mirror, she could see Pop amble out of the concrete building with his hands stuck in his overall pockets.

"What can I do for you?"

Ashton rolled down her window and looked directly at him a few seconds without speaking. She could see a glimmer of recognition flicker across his face. "Ten dollars of regular ought to do it," she said finally. She leaned out the window and watched as he pumped the gas. "I was in here on Monday, remember?"

The look of indifference had settled back onto his face. "Lots of folks come through here."

"You told me a story about how the white squirrels got to Fox Run," she reminded him.

"Did I now?" His attention remained focused on the pump meter.

"I told you that I was from West Virginia, and you were surprised. You seemed to think that I was from around here." She knew her questions were pointless. His attention did not need jarring. He was purposely avoiding her.

Pop spit a stream of tobacco juice behind him. "If you say I did, then I reckon I must have. But I can't for the life of me remember." He screwed the cap back on the tank. "Check under the hood?"

"No, thanks." She handed him a ten. "You told me I looked like a girl who used to live here."

Pop shook his head. His expression remained blank. "Sorry."

Ashton hopped out of the truck and followed him back around the service island. "I need to know that girl's name." Her hand caught his shirt sleeve. "Please, you must help me. What is the name of the girl I look like?"

Pop took a few steps away, then turned back around. His wrinkles furrowed. "You listen to me, young lady. Take the advice of somebody that knows what he's talking about. Let sleeping dogs lie!"

Ashton stared after him. His advice had taken her by surprise. The click of the lock on his door after he had gone inside said the rest. He wanted to be left alone!

She got back in the truck and drove away. She was going to find out the name of her look-alike if it took all day. She wondered how many people she would have to offend in the process.

There was an empty parking space right in front of Varner's. Ashton whipped into it and parked. She checked the time. It was a quarter to two. The lunchtime crowd should have already thinned out.

Except for a young couple in the back, the grill was empty. Ashton sat down at the soda fountain. She picked up one of the plastic menus and waited until Myra was standing in front of her before lowering it from her face.

"Hello, Myra."

The waitress was quick to collect herself. "What can I get for you, honey?"

"How about a cherry coke?"

Myra set a plastic cup down in front of her a few minutes later. "I, uh, I sort of figured you'd be back."

Ashton stirred her drink with the straw. "You did?"

"I guess you want to know why I told you to stay away from Hamp Breyer," she stammered.

Ashton sipped her coke but said nothing.

Myra's chuckle was not convincing. "I guess I was just mad at Mr. Breyer for embarrassing me in front of all my customers. I hope I didn't upset you," she added hurriedly.

"Not at all." Ashton locked onto Myra's gaze and refused to let go. The waitress was lying, and both of them knew it.

"Anything else?" Myra asked, reaching under the counter.

Ashton's stare did not waver. "You can tell me the name of the woman I look like."

Myra sponged the counter. Her eyes stayed fixed on the formica.

"Someone is trying to scare me out of town," Ashton persisted. "I would at least like to know why."

The waitress accepted the news without a flinch. Ashton was certain that her announcement had come as no great surprise.

"Ashley. Ashley Kiel." Myra let out a deep breath that sounded like a heavy sigh of relief.

Ashton repeated the name. Had Molly not called her Ashley? "Why should my resemblance to this woman make me the target of some lunatic?"

"Can't say."

Ashton refused to let Myra shrink away from her gaze. "Can't or won't?"

"Leave well enough alone," she rasped between clinched teeth.

The bell from the kitchen sounded.

Myra turned to pick up her next order.

"Don't go opening up old wounds, honey," the waitress told her gently on her way back to the couple in the booth.

Ashton left the grill in a hurry. There was one person who could provide her with answers. The sweet little lady had deceived her already, but that had been before Ashton knew the right questions to ask.

Ashton made herself comfortable in the sitting room of the *Red Fox Inn.* She declined Molly's offer of hot chocolate and oatmeal cookies and decided to get straight to the point. "Tell me about Ashley Kiel."

Molly's dimples stopped dancing. Wrinkles arched around her mouth. "Where did you hear that name?"

Ashton knew she had struck a nerve. "I understand that's the name of the woman I'm supposed to look so much like." Her tone softened. "You knew that all along, didn't you, Molly? You even called me Ashley the first time you saw me. Remember? I thought you had just misunderstood my name."

Molly made no attempt to deny it. "Why on earth would you be interested in her?"

"I'm curious," she said without blinking.

"Curious?"

Ashton nodded. At first she hadn't planned on telling Molly the whole story. Now, she knew she had no alternative. "Someone is trying to run me out of town. I want to know why. I think it has something to do with my resembling this Kiel woman."

"Trying to run you out of town?" echoed the old woman. "Dear me." Her palm stroked her cheek. "Something else has happened since you went up to Cav's place?"

Ashton sat on the edge of the settee. "You knew my room hadn't been plundered by pranksters or some kook on the loose, didn't you?"

Molly waited a few moments before speaking. "I thought you'd be safe with Cav."

"Pilfering the guest room was just the beginning."

Molly began rocking faster.

Ashton continued, leaning closer to her friend. "Someone has been taking potshots at me."

Molly's hand shot to her mouth.

"One of them almost killed Cav's dog," she continued. "This morning, Cav and I took his plane up and had to limp back in on one engine. One of the oil lines had been loosened."

Ashton relaxed back against the velvet cushion. She waited for Molly to volunteer some remark that would help solve the mystery. She was prepared to wait all day if need be.

Molly tucked the afghan tighter around her legs. She looked Ashton right in the eye. "I swear, I don't know who's doing this to you."

"Have you any idea why?" pressed Ashton.

Molly shook her head. Her gaze settled on the pink and purple squares covering her lap. "I'd help you if I could, Ashton."

"Maybe the person responsible has a grudge to settle, and they're mistaking me for her," she wondered aloud. "Perhaps I could meet her."

"Meet who?"

"Why, Ashley, of course."

"I'm afraid that's impossible." Molly ceased rocking. "Ashley's dead."

"Dead?" Ashton was stunned. It was as though she had just learned of the death of a friend. Her likeness to Ashley had created a special bond. "How?" she inquired a moment later.

"An automobile accident. Poor dear. It was such a tragedy." Her voice began to quaver. "She was no older than you."

"No older than I?" she repeated. "I guess that explains why I've startled some of the townspeople."

Molly nodded. "Probably so. You two look enough alike to be twins."

Ashton frowned. "But it still doesn't explain why someone would want me out of town because of that resemblance." She looked up suddenly. "What did you just say? Just a moment ago."

"I said that the two of you could almost pass for twins."

"Twins?" gulped Ashton. Twins, she repeated to herself. The two names were similar. Perhaps . . .

"Where could I find Ashley's relatives?"

Molly shrugged. "There are none. At least, none that I know about."

"Her folks?"

"Deceased."

"How about brothers, or sisters?" she asked hopefully.

Molly thought for several moments. "She was an only child. I'm certain."

"Oh." Ashton sunk back against the settee. "How about a husband?"

"She wasn't married."

"Is there anything else you can tell me about Ashley?" she asked, almost pleading. "I have to know who's harassing me and why. Ashley's my only clue."

Molly's finger tapped against her chin. "I'm afraid I can't help you there, dear."

"Neither could Pop or Myra," Ashton said dejectedly.

"Oh, what did they tell you?"

"They quoted mountain philosophy to me," she answered, half smiling. "One told me to let sleeping dogs lie; the other said not to open up old wounds."

"It seems they weren't any more help than I." Molly patted Ashton's knee. "I'm so sorry. If I should think of anything else, I'll call. I promise." She stifled a yawn. "Dear me. I'm more fatigued than I thought." She stood up slowly. Her fingers gripped the arms of the rocker as she rose. "I thought for sure I could get by without my after-lunch snooze. I reckon I was wrong. Excuse me, dear?"

"Of course." Ashton forced a smile. She had difficulty believing that Molly had to take regular afternoon naps.

Ashton locked the front door of the inn on her way out. Her chat with Molly had accomplished nothing. It was obvious that the old lady remembered a lot more than she cared to admit. For that matter, so did Pop and Myra! No one was talking! It was apparent that not one of the three had any intention of opening up to her. Why? she wondered over and over on her way back through Fox Run. What kind of power could a dead woman possibly exert over those three? What could Ashley have done that was so terrible? Could she have hurt someone so badly that the person would strike out against someone who looked like her? Surely the person trying to hurt her knew that Ashley was dead.

Ashton caught her breath. Suppose that person had been responsible for the automobile accident. Her fingers froze around the steering wheel. What if her being in town were a haunting reminder for the one who had committed such a horrible act?

Ashton drove back up the mountain to *Wolf Lair* even more confused than she had been upon leaving Molly's. It seemed that everywhere she turned for information on Ashley Kiel, she ran into one dead-end after another.

No birth or death certificate had ever been filed for her in the courthouse. She had no police record, had never registered to vote or applied for a driver's license. According to the tax collector's office, there were no records of her ever owning, buying, selling, or inheriting property in Transylvania County. Neither the telephone company nor the post office had any records of telephone listings or addresses for her or for any other Kiel.

Ashton was totally baffled. There were no legal documents to prove that Ashley had ever existed in Fox Run.

"Hey there, Silver Wolf. You got your ears on?" clipped a voice over the CB.

Ashton picked up the mike. "You got the Silver Wolf. . . . Come back. . . . Sorry, no copy." She played with the squelch button. The static disappeared. "You got the Silver Wolf. Come back. . . . Cav, is that you?"

"Time's running out for you, gal," drawled a man's voice over the receiver. "You copy?" he chuckled.

"Who is this?" she demanded. She waited. There was no answer. "You make sure you copy this loud and clear, mister," she said angrily. "If you have something to say to me, be man enough to say it to my face!" With that, she flipped off the CB.

Ashton looked into the side mirrors. There was no one behind her. She couldn't remember having passed any cars at all in the last fifteen minutes. She was frightened! But she had been determined not to let it show in her voice.

That jerk had probably had her in his sight all day, just like those days on the mountain. He was probably gloating this very minute over how clever he was to have gone undetected. Ashton gripped the wheel tighter as she skidded around a curve. More than anything, she was furious. How dare he bully her!

It took a few minutes for her to collect herself. When she had, she took the curves slower and loosened her hold on the steering wheel. Keeping her wits about her was the only way she'd be able to outsmart that character, she decided. When he was ready to make his next move, she'd be waiting. He had intimidated her long enough. Still fuming, Ashton cut onto *Wolf Lair* property.

Cav came barreling down the mountain ahead of her.

She stopped and waited for him.

His vehicle careened to a stop beside the truck.

Cav leaned out the window, "You okay?"

Ashton nodded. She could tell by his anxious expression that he had picked up the message, too. "I'm okay. More angry than anything else. That creep is probably still laughing!"

"Not for long!" he assured her, his fists balled. "I tried to raise you on the radio. Why didn't you answer? I was worried."

Ashton felt her mouth relaxing into a grin. "I cut that damn thing off!"

"You're one gutsy lady!" He flashed her one of his lop-sided grins. "Meet you back up at the house."

"Get packed?" Ashton wasn't sure she had heard him correctly a few minutes later as they walked up onto the porch. "What do you mean, 'Let's get packed'?"

Cav opened the door. "Shall we discuss this inside where it's warm?"

Shivering, Ashton refused to budge from the steps. "If you think I'm leaving here before I find out what's been going on, you're nuts!" A second later, she burst out laughing. She had a feeling she must look pretty ridiculous. Her hands were planted defiantly on her hips; her legs were parted as though she were poised for a fight. "Feel free to butt in at any time," she grinned, feeling like a brat who had just thrown a temper tantrum.

"Good thing you said that. I was just getting ready to turn you across my knee." Cav sat down on the step and patted the space beside him. "That's better." He squeezed her close. "Now before you start tearing into me again, please remember that I said, 'Let's get packed.' Let's—as in 'let us.' Plural. Understand?"

She eyed him suspiciously. "You're not going to say something stupid like, let me take you away from all this, are you?"

Cav traced an "x" on his chest. "Cross my heart. I have business to attend to up in Asheville, and I thought you might like to go along."

She still wasn't convinced. "So why'd you wait until now to mention it?"

"The fellow from the restaurant supply house called me a couple of hours ago. I haven't seen you since lunch, remember?" He tousled her curls. "What do you say? After my appointment, we could do a little sightseeing, go out for dinner, a little dancing." He hugged her closer.

Her lips brushed against his neck. "Who was it who said I can resist all but temptation?"

"I have no idea," Cav answered, pulling her to her feet, "but whoever said it sounds like my kind of philosopher!"

Chapter Twelve

A CARILLON chimed the five o'clock hour. Across the Asheville city green, the last of the visitors to Thomas Wolfe's home filed out of the rooming house where the author had spent his boyhood. Low-hanging clouds hovered above the park, threatening to flurry snow across the statues and monuments presiding there.

Ashton huddled closer to Cav. His broad shoulders blocked her from the wind that sliced across the square. She knew that she should be annoyed with him, but she just didn't have the heart. Besides, she told herself, leaving Fox Run for the weekend had given her just the change she needed to regroup and develop a strategy for her next move.

She stole a glimpse at the man beside her. More importantly, she reminded herself, the trip had given her the opportunity to spend more wonderful hours with Cav. She had a sneaking suspicion that this last fact was even more important to her than baiting the weirdo who was after her!

Ashton smiled up at his ruggedly handsome face. "What happened to all that pressing business you told me about yesterday?" she couldn't resist asking.

Cav tossed a handful of peanuts into a covey of pigeons that had congregated around the bench across from where they sat. "I'm tending to it right now."

"What? Feeding the birds? Or babysitting me?" she asked, teasing.

He chuckled.

Ashton buried her chin in the fleece collar of his jacket. "You know, Mr. Cavanaugh, you didn't strike me as the sort of man who had to resort to deception to get what he wanted."

"That's not my usual nature," he agreed solemnly.

The heat of his breath warmed the chill of her bones far better than the hot rum toddy they had shared a few minutes earlier after they had strolled down cobblestone lanes in Asheville's restored section.

"I hear that love makes a man do crazy things," he said without taking his eyes off the pigeons.

His words sent Ashton's emotions spiraling to an all-time high. "You mean like sitting in the park in below-freezing weather feeding pigeons?" she ventured quietly.

He kissed the tip of her nose. "How'd you know?"

Her eyes were bright enough to light the entire city. "Because that's the way I feel, and I love you, too."

"I know." His arms tightened around her ribs. "What woman in her right mind wouldn't?"

"Oh, you!" she exclaimed, belting him in the stomach.

He caught hold of her hand. "Watch it, lady, or I'll turn you over my knee and teach you a lesson or two."

She wound her arms around his neck and pressed herself as close as their jackets would allow. "You keep threatening to do that, but you never do." Her lips feathered across his.

Cav clasped her even tighter and reclaimed her mouth with a fiery passion.

Ashton devoured him. His kisses could thaw an ice maiden. Already, he had her hungering for the privacy of their suite.

"How'd Sid take the news that you'd be staying on a few days?" asked Cav as they crossed the street to the Inn on the Plaza.

She looped her arm through his. "He grunted and

snorted a little, but I don't think he's started taking appli-
cations for my replacement yet."

"Too bad!" he remarked. His big hand fitted to her
waist. "Wolf Lair sure could use its own resident geologist."

Sparks flew within her. She felt tall enough to pluck the
gray, ruffled clouds from the sky. Ashton said nothing as
they walked through the lobby; she didn't trust herself to
speak. Not just yet. Five days wasn't long enough to nur-
ture the kind of relationship she dreamed of for herself and
Cav. Or was it, she asked herself as the elevator stopped on
the sixteenth floor.

Cav unlocked the door to their room and motioned her
inside. He helped her out of her coat, then bundled his
arms around her. One of his hands found a soft curve and
squeezed it gently. "Ummm. I have a notion to keep you
hostage right here all next week."

Her lips started at his chin and nibbled their way to his
ear. "You can't. You have a resort to open."

"That's right! How could I have forgotten!" Hot breath
filtered through her curls. "Maybe I should postpone the
opening a week or two."

"Don't you dare!" she exclaimed, nipping at his neck.
"I've already confirmed my reservation for the grand
opening."

Masterful fingers lifted her sweater and slipped underneath to begin massaging the hollow of her back. "You
don't need a reservation. As a matter of fact, you don't
even need to leave."

Ashton kicked off her shoes and dropped down onto the
sofa. "Maybe you should tell that to the guy who's determined to get me out of town."

"You just wait until I get hold of that bastard. I'll tell
him a hell of a lot more than that," he promised, sealing
his vow with a kiss. "He'll regret ever looking twice in
your direction when I get through with him."

"I don't care how you tear, spindle, or mutilate him, just
as long as I get to throw the first punch." She smiled se-

cretly. She had never required her own Sir Galahad to fight her battles, but with Cav volunteering for the job, she might just make an exception.

"It's a deal. Of course, Zebo might want to argue with you." Cav kicked his legs over the end of the couch and rested his head in her lap. "Has the name Kiel rung any kind of bell for you yet?"

"Not even a tingle," she sighed. Her lack of success in locating anyone who even had the same last name as Ashley frustrated her. "If it weren't for some of the townspeople being in such a tizzy because I look like her, I'd dismiss the possibility that she even existed."

Cav frowned. "From what you've told me, she didn't exist—at least, not legally."

"That's what bothers me." She absently massaged his temples. "I'm beginning to wonder if maybe some concerned citizen didn't go to great lengths to cover up the fact that Ashley even lived in Fox Run."

"It's possible," agreed Cav. "If that's the case, though, she must have been involved in something that the good people of Fox Run would just as soon forget."

"I just wish I could find out what she did that was so terrible," Ashton remarked anxiously. "Maybe that would give me a clue to the identity of that lunatic!"

"I'm surprised Molly wasn't more of a help," he told her.

"So am I. She told me just enough to answer my questions but not enough to satisfy my curiosity." Ashton's brows knitted together. "Her every answer was so guarded. I couldn't get her to elaborate on any of her remarks."

"I can't understand that, either," he said, folding his hands across his chest. "Usually, Molly rambles on and on for hours." Cav shifted his weight so he could look directly at her. "Hey, do you think you could have been related to Ashley in some way?"

Ashton cocooned herself between him and the corner of the sofa. "I thought about that, too," she said reluctantly, "but Molly said Ashley had no brothers or sisters."

"Maybe you're cousins," he suggested. "Sometimes they can look as much alike as sisters."

Ashton frowned. Until yesterday, she had regarded her past identify with little more than a casual curiosity. But now . . . It might just be possible that she had stumbled across her roots quite by accident.

Stop it! she cautioned herself. She simply could not allow herself to pursue such thoughts. She was a scientist. It was her nature to rely on logic and deductive reasoning to seek answers for the unknown. Perplexing matters were not dismissed as mere coincidences. The odds of her winning the Irish Sweepstakes were more in her favor than the possibility of having found long-lost relatives in Transylvania County.

"You know, it isn't inconceivable that you might have distant relatives in this part of North Carolina," Cav said, reading her thoughts.

She shook her head. "I refuse to allow myself even to consider that possibility."

"I don't care whether you believe in fate or not. I do," he announced.

"Why do you say that?"

Cav pulled her head down even with his. His eyes had a gleam with the sparkle of a fine diamond. "Because Lady Luck sure had my best interests at heart when she brought you to Fox Run."

She melted at the look in his eyes. Mesmerized, she lowered her mouth to his. At first, his lips caressed hers, then his tongue took searing possession. Flames of passion burned deep inside both of them.

Ashton was transferred from the sofa to the bed in one swift motion.

Tiny kisses peppered down her neck and over cashmere mounds in quest of the treasures cached within.

Ashton smiled a slow, satisfied smile. They hadn't removed the *Do Not Disturb* sign until well after lunch. She ran her fingers through his hair. "I thought you promised me a night out on the town."

Manly fingers dug into her soft flesh. "I did," he said, his hands firm around her waist. "Our reservations aren't for another couple of hours." He nuzzled her sweater up with his nose and planted kisses along her midriff.

"What happened to all that sightseeing we were going to do?" she reminded him.

Her fingers began to grip his dark shocks. His mouth still played above her waist, but one hand had unzippered her slacks and its fingers were teasing beneath her bikini. "All the sights worth seeing are right in this room," he murmured against her skin.

She knew she could refuse him nothing. "Hmmm. Whatever you say." At that instant, the only feast she wanted was the many delicious courses his body had to offer.

Cashmere and wool vanished so quickly, she wondered if the longing vaulting inside her had willed away her clothes. Her breasts jutted out to him, pleading for his caress. He cupped the satiny globes, one in each hand. Their peaks hardened like pebbles under his kisses.

His tongue flicked across her, leaving no part hungry. Every inch of her came instantly alive. No fuse was left undetonated.

They came together in a rush of desire that left them both gasping for air. Legs embraced legs; soft bosom came hard against firm chest. Man and woman, they were as one. The same urgency flowed out of his veins and into hers.

Cav reclaimed what was his with thrusts that were deep and demanding. He moved as though he possessed a sixth sense that told him her every want and need before she felt them herself. One moment, his touch was hypnotic. The next, she quaked and trembled from the shock waves of pleasure he was sending through her.

The room spun round and round. Each revolution made her dizzier and dizzier. Her mouth shaped his name, but the strength to utter the sound could not be found.

Ashton flung herself closer and closer, blinded, deaf to all but their gasps and groans. Her cells were exploding, in her brain, her toes, her nipples, her belly. Cav flung himself deeper, and she was sent hurtling toward ecstasy.

"Why don't we just have room service send up a tray?" yawned Cav a little later.

"Nothing doing, buster. You promised to wine and dine me, and I intend to hold you to it." She escaped from the sweet confines of his arms, laughing. "Just because you've had your way with me does not mean you can deny me decent treatment."

"What if I refuse?"

She eluded his attempts to recapture her. "Then you'll just have to suffer the consequences."

"Which are?" he asked, propping himself up on his elbow.

Ashton smiled sweetly. "Horrors and pains so excruciating, just talking about them would make you violently ill."

"Women!" His head plopped back down onto the pillow. "There has to be an easier way!"

"Think so, huh?" She threw back the covers and capered out of bed. She struck a provocative pose. "Have you thought what the alternatives might be?"

He tossed her the oxford-striped shirt he had been wearing earlier. "Get some clothes on, will you? Having to resist temptation twenty-four hours a day is wearing me out!"

She hooked the shirt over her shoulder and walked into the dressing room. Suppressing her giggles was harder than exaggerating the swing of her hips.

Sighing contendedly, she slid down into a tub brimming with hot, lavender scented bubbles. Sweetness flooded her weary limbs. Every time they made love proved more thrilling than the last. Cav's prowess as a lover was unrivaled. With nothing to prove and no selfish intentions motivating him, he dedicated hour after hour to exploring and arousing and giving more pleasure and fulfillment than she had ever thought possible. His moves could not have been more perfect had he been following a detailed guide to lovemaking. She sighed, remembering his kisses.

Ashton sank deeper and deeper into the perfumed suds. She happily reenacted in her mind the fastasy-come-true she had just experienced. Her lips were tweaked with a smile that had only recently been cultivated. There was no doubt in her mind who was responsible for its presence. In six short days, Cav had become a wonderful, intricate part of her life. An existence without him would be only tolerable at best. In the past, she had never given a second thought to her arrangement of priorities. Her career had always taken precedence over all else. What men friends she had always took a back seat to her own goals. All that had changed! Now, she was even beginning to wonder if her work were still the know-all, end-all, cure-all it had once been.

"Shake a leg, babe," Cav called. "We've got less than half an hour to make our reservation."

"Be right with you." Ashton stepped out of the tub with her towel wrapped around her. "All yours," she said as she opened the door.

A muscular frame that was without an ounce of fat blocked her exit. "I'll take it. For sure."

She ducked under his arm. "The bathroom, lover boy."

He lunged at her.

She sidestepped away before he could tackle her. "Thirty minutes. Remember?"

A safe distance away, she pretended to be absorbed in selecting her attire for the evening. A subtle tug at the knot and the towel slithered down her legs. She blew Cav a kiss over her shoulder, then pointed to the shower. "Ta, ta."

Chapter Thirteen

Two HOURS later, lounging in a plush velvet chair and sipping vintage chardonnay from a Waterford goblet, Ashton felt as though she were sitting on top of the world. The restaurant was posh and romantic, the cuisine gourmet, and her escort handsome, witty, and ever so attentive. She hoped she looked only half as glamorous as she felt. Her dress had started her purring the minute she wiggled into it, and she hadn't stopped purring yet. Cut straight and in the style of a slip, the outfit was made of soft angora. Even hanging on the rack, the dress had looked all cuddly and kittenish, and that was exactly how she felt at that moment with the fluffy fur clinging to all her curves. The side slits reaching from her calves to midway up her thighs showed off the shapely, well-exercised products of many years of hiking and horseback riding. The color, a champagne beige, darkened her flawless skin a shade more than its natural, year-round tan.

Usually not one to buy on a whim, she had seen the dress in the window of a haute couture boutique and had rushed in to buy it before Cav returned from the antique shop where he had left his keys. She had been certain it would knock his eyes out, and she had been so, so right! His gaze had hardly strayed from her once during the oysters gratinee and the rack of lamb. His eyes had raked over her so many times, she had lost count. Her broker might disagree, but this dress had been a great investment. It was undoubtedly worth every dollar of its three-digit price tag.

Passion-charged looks crossed over the candle tops. The gleam in her eyes played in the glow of his. Nothing—not the tuxedo-clad waiters, the Royal Doulton setting atop Irish linen, the bird's-eye view of Asheville from the forty-fourth floor—could even begin to impress her as much as the man opposite her. He looked just as confident and comfortable in his french cuffs and tailor-made suit as he did in his flannels and levis—and just as enticing!

Ashton wondered why he had not followed some of his colleagues onto the television screen and into magazine advertisements. He possessed a raw sensuality that could send women to the stores in droves to purchase whatever product he chose to endorse.

"Look who just walked in," said Cav, nodding to the door a short while later. "Ol' Hamp's playing with the big-leaguers now."

Ashton slanted a look in the direction Cav was indicating. Hampton and Judith Breyer, along with a group of a dozen or so other couples, were waiting to be seated.

Cav leaned closer to her. "The guy on his left is the Lieutenant Governor, and the loud fellow behind him is the Attorney General."

"That's some entourage," she remarked, returning her attention to her companion. "I would imagine that with elections only three days away, they've all been doing some heavy campaigning this weekend."

She glanced up from Cav's face a moment later when the maitre d' led Breyer's party past their table. Breyer and Judith brought up the rear as the group filed by. Ashton delivered an affable smile in their direction. Judith looked right through her as though she had never seen her before. Hampton was aware of her, but he gave her an impersonal nod that could have been intended for any stranger in the room.

"What do you suppose is wrong with them?" she wondered aloud, her gaze following them to their table. "Judith ignored us, and Hamp acted like he didn't even recognize us." She took a sip of the chardonnay. "After that incident with Zebo, he had me convinced that he was a likeable person who just had trouble with human company." She frowned to herself. "Now I'm beginning to wonder."

"Maybe the pressures of the campaign are getting to him," Cav suggested.

"Perhaps." Her eyes cut to the table where the group had been seated. Breyer and his sister both looked so stiff and formal that Ashton couldn't help but laugh. "Maybe when he's in his political element, he has to maintain a certain aloofness for appearance's sake. I guess that goes for Judith, too," she added when Breyer's sister failed to acknowledge her smile for the second time. "I believe I liked them both much better when they didn't have to project any sort of image at all."

Cav moved his chair closer to hers. Large, strong fingers wove themselves through smaller ones. "I don't know what kind of image you're trying to project," he said, his voice hoarse and throaty, "but that dress would get my vote any day." His cheek brushed hers. "So would what's in it."

Ashton shook her hair back from around her face. "Too bad I'm not running for office."

"What do you mean? Too bad? I'm relieved!" He nipped teasingly at the flesh hidden under the cascade of curls. "Having to share you with anyone else would be more than I could endure!"

The flicker in his eyes reflected hers. Ashton had a feeling the evening was going to be much shorter than planned.

"How about some dessert?" he asked when the last of the wine had been finished.

Ashton laughed. "Thanks, but no thanks. One more bite, and I'll split these seams for sure."

"That in itself would be some treat!" He motioned for

the waiter, explaining to Ashton that he had to keep up his strength.

"By all means," she chuckled.

The pastry chef rolled the dessert cart over to their table and explained in great detail each of the gooey choices. While Cav was trying to make up his mind between the Grand Marnier soufflé, and the mocha mousse parfait, Ashton excused herself.

"I'll only be a minute," she said when he helped her out of her chair.

Cav grinned his wonderfully lopsided grin. "I'll be counting the seconds!"

Ashton walked into the lounge and was surprised to see Judith standing at the mirror tucking stray strands of her coal black hair back into the neat little chignon at the nape of her neck.

"Hello, Judith," she greeted cheerfully, walking up next to her.

The face in the mirror all but froze. Its cheeks reddened a shade deeper than her tunic. "Good evening," returned Judith, her words as stiff as her body.

Ashton rummaged through her clutch, uncomfortably aware that heavily made-up eyes were probing her face with searing glances. Judith's coolness seemed deliberate but Ashton was at a loss for the reason. Breyer's sister had been quite chummy the first of the week and had even suggested they meet for lunch. Four days later, the woman would barely acknowledge her presence.

Ashton decided her best defense would be to act as though nothing were wrong. "You certainly look lovely," she said as she began outlining her lips with a rosewood glaze. "That outfit is elegant! The color's perfect for you." She paused and waited for a reply. When none came, she continued. "You must be very proud of your brother. I understand he's a shoo-in for the State Senate."

"Why don't you just cut the chit-chat!" Judith snapped her purse shut. "You don't give a damn about how I look or about Hamp's career. We both know why you're here."

Ashton's mouth dropped open. "What are you talking about?"

Judith said nothing. She just glared at her.

"Are you alright? You look awfully flushed." Ashton reached for her arm. "Here, I'll help you over to the sofa. Perhaps if you sat down a moment."

Long nails lashed out at her.

Ashton pulled back, stunned.

"I know what you're doing here." Judith's tone and her eyes had the same dull glaze. "You may have fooled Hamp, but you can't fool me."

Ashton did her best to remain calm. "I'm not trying to fool either you or your brother," she said gently. "If I've done something to upset you, please let me know, and we can talk about it."

Judith continued as though she had heard nothing. "I know all about your kind. You're just waiting for the chance to sink your claws into my brother, aren't you? I know how you are. She was the same way."

"She?" repeated Ashton, even more confused. She hesitated for a moment, then decided she had nothing to lose by playing out her hunch. "You're angry at me because of Ashley Kiel, aren't you?"

Judith looked as though she had been slapped in the face. There was fury in her eyes, but her voice was barely audible. "How dare you mention that tramp's name in my presence."

Ashton knew instantly that she had hit a nerve. "You hated her, didn't you?" she asked, hoping to draw out information on the mystery woman.

"I loathed her," she answered calmly. "I absolutely loathed the woman!"

"Why?" pressed Ashton, certain that at any minute Judith would explode.

"She was nothing but trouble to my—"

The door to the lounge swung open. Judith stopped in mid-sentence. A woman who looked like she had been poured into her black knit dress walked in.

"Are you feeling better, dear?" she asked Judith. "Hamp asked me to come check on you."

Judith's manner changed as rapidly as a chameleon switches colors, and she once again became the picture of charm and poise. "Why, I'm just fine, Becky Lee. Too much champagne, I suppose. I know I shouldn't drink on an empty stomach, but I never could resist a celebration." Her voice was honey-coated. "You're real sweet to come and see about me."

Judith then reached for Ashton's arm. Ashton thought she was about to introduce her to the Attorney General's wife. Instead, she gave her elbow a tight squeeze before releasing it. "That dress certainly is stunning. Do give Cav my love, dear," she said sweetly as she breezed past.

Ashton was no less confounded when she and Cav returned to their suite after discoing past midnight. She could find no explanation to rationalize Judith's behavior. She supposed the woman could have been drunk. That would account for her sharp tongue. Still, she had seemed in complete control of her faculties.

"You would not have believed her," she told Cav after recounting again what had happened in the ladies' room. "She was a real schizo! One minute, she was breathing fire. The next, she was chatting away like we were Friday morning bridge partners."

"Sounds to me like she thinks you've got an eye on her brother," offered Cav, loosening his tie.

Ashton agreed. "That's the impression I got, too. But even if I were out to get him, I can't understand why she should be so possessive." She stuffed a pillow behind her back and settled against the headboard. "You should have seen her when I mentioned Ashley Kiel. I thought for sure she was going to pounce on me and claw my eyes out." She paused a few seconds and said nothing. "You know," continued Ashton, sliding the rosebud along the chain. "I'd be willing to bet that Hampton and Ashley were romantically involved at one time, and that's the scandal that everyone is so tight-lipped about."

Cav stretched out beside her. "You might have something there."

"I'll just bet I do!" she declared confidently. "Breyer has access to all the courthouse files, so that might explain why there are no records of Ashley ever even living in Fox Run." Deep in thought, she fell back against his arm. "There just might have been something in those records that could have linked the two of them together," she reflected aloud. "Something that could put an end to any political aspirations he might have. Maybe I should have a little chat with him when I get back to town," she mused.

Cav shook his head. "I doubt if that would do any good."

"Why not?"

He guided her head down onto his shoulder. "Because if he did go to all that trouble to cover his tracks, he's not going to admit to it now," he pointed out.

"You're probably right," she sighed, molding herself as close to him as she could. "Too bad the one person who could answer my questions won't."

"Molly?"

She nodded. "I just know there's a lot more than what she's telling me. When I visited her yesterday, I had a feeling she was on the verge of opening up to me right before she excused herself."

"Maybe that's why she invented the story about her afternoon nap," he suggested, cuddling her close. "Perhaps she was afraid of saying too much, and she knew she would if she continued talking to you about it."

"I should visit her again," she thought out loud. "After all, she's lived in Fox Run over seventy years. If anybody knows the town's secrets, it would be her." Ashton felt better already. Molly would help her. She just had to.

"Of course, there's nothing I can do about it right now," Ashton said. Nimble fingers skied down Cav's shirt unfastening buttons en route. Curly tendrils sprang out to greet her. "Right now, I believe there might just be more pressing matters at hand." Her teeth nipped gently at his chest. "Matters which need my immediate, undivided attention." She could tell by Cav's quick breaths that he was in complete agreement.

"Did I ever tell you what an absolute knock-out you are in that little number?" he asked, showering kisses down her neck and across her shoulders.

"Several times." Her arms found their way around his neck. She arched herself against him. "One more time wouldn't hurt."

His chin slid the strap of angora off her shoulder. "I think I like it best, though, when you're wearing nothing at all," he whispered huskily.

Her contours fit perfectly with his. She would have been content to remain in that position all night. "What about that slinky nightgown I brought?" she asked when he slid her dress the rest of the way down her length.

"It's going to look real pretty hanging on the bedpost." His mouth hungrily covered hers.

"Who am I to complain?" she asked, lying back to enjoy herself.

Ashton remained alert long after Cav's breathing had settled back into its quiet, regular pattern. Even while he slept, his arms were locked around her as though he were trying to reassure himself of her presence.

Smiling softly, Ashton closed her eyes. There was no question about it: she could spend the rest of her days held snugly in his arms.

Chapter Fourteen

Ashton huddled beside Cav in the pickup and waited for some sign of life to appear inside the *Red Fox Inn.* The twenty minutes they had sat there seemed like two hours. The door finally opened, and Molly stepped out in her housecoat to retrieve the Sunday morning paper from the porch. When she saw the *Wolf Lair* truck parked in her driveway, she waved to them as though she had expected to open her door at eight o'clock and find them there.

"I'm awfully sorry to be troubling you this early," she told Molly as the old lady hung their coats in the foyer. "I know I should have called first, but I need to talk to you, and it just can't wait any longer."

Molly's smile was sincere. "I know, honey. I've been needing to talk to you, too, since you left on Friday." She smoothed dark curls away from Ashton's face. "I tried calling you all weekend, but you weren't home." She motioned them into the sitting room. "Please. Go in and make yourselves comfortable. I'll fix us some coffee. Build us a fire, will you, Cav?" she called on her way into the kitchen. "This old house is getting mighty drafty."

Ashton walked around the parlor with Sebastian padding along beside her. The room had a cozy warmth about it that made her feel at home every time she was in it; she had noticed that her first visit there. She stopped at the credenza to admire Molly's collection of music boxes. The pony carousel fascinated her! She could not resist the urge to lift it from its place. The ponies turned and the tune played as though they were doing so of their own accord. "Rhapsody in Blue" always prompted a surge of pleasant feelings. She wished she could remember why.

"I'm so sorry I was under the weather on Friday," apologized Molly as she served coffee and hot buttered buns. "It must have been a touch of the flu."

Ashton sat down beside Cav. "That's alright. I understand," she assured her.

Molly stared down at her coffee. "Well, you shouldn't," she said suddenly. "The truth of the matter is that I just plain didn't want to continue our talk."

Ashton smiled. "I know that. I'll bet you've never had to take an afternoon nap in your life."

Molly didn't crack a smile. Her head remained downcast.

Ashton was concerned. Molly hadn't looked like she was under the weather on Friday, but she certainly did now. Her face was tired and drawn. Her eyes had lost their luster. Worst of all, she looked as if her age were finally catching up with her.

Cav, too, was aware of her poor spirits. "Molly, are you sure you're okay?" he asked. "If you don't feel like company, we can come back later."

"I'm fine. Don't go worrying about me." Her words were flat.

Ashton knew that if her elderly friend were really feeling fine, she would have snapped to answer Cav's question with a reply that she was fit as a fiddle. "Perhaps we should come back later," she told Cav softly.

Molly's voice finally lifted. "Don't you dare, young lady. Our chat is long enough overdue as it is."

"Then you'll tell me everything you know about Ashley Kiel?"

"I swear I'll answer any question you might have." Her chair stopped rocking. "But first of all, you have to answer me a question."

Ashton nodded.

Molly hesitated for a moment before continuing. "Tell me the real reason you've come to Fox Run."

Ashton was confused. "The real reason? I thought I had explained all that to you on Monday."

The old lady nodded impatiently. "I know what you told me. All about being a geologist and how you'd come to Fox Run to investigate some kind of a metal. What was it?"

Ashton was quick to provide the name.

"Yes. That's it. Gallium." Molly took a deep breath. Her hands clasped together. "Please, dear, you must tell me the truth. It's very important that I know now before we proceed any further. Why did you come here?"

"Everything I told you before was true. I did come here on a mining project." She could sense that she had still not convinced Molly of that. "Why don't you believe me? I have no reason to lie to you."

"Were you sent here?" queried Molly. "Or did you come of your own choosing?"

Ashton failed to see the relevance of that question. Still, she knew if she wanted the information about Ashley, she would have to humor Molly. "Actually, I selected myself for the job."

Molly's nod was a knowing one. "I see. Go on."

"I discovered recently that I miss being in the field," she answered, not knowing exactly what kind of an answer she was expected to give. "When the chance came to investigate gallium potential in western North Carolina, I took the assignment myself rather than pass it on to one of my staff."

"Is that all?"

Ashton exchanged puzzled looks with Cav. "Should there be more?" she asked.

"Please. Just bear with me a moment longer," requested Molly. "Did you know the exact location beforehand? Did you know that you would be coming specifically to Fox Run?"

Ashton chuckled. "I decided that this particular assignment was the one I wanted because the name Fox Run has such a quaint sound to it. The name alone would encourage visitors, if only out of curiosity."

"Is it as quaint as you had expected?"

Ashton nodded. "It's exactly as I thought it would be."

Molly patted her lap. Sebastian jumped onto it. She stroked her calico cat for the longest while. "Alright, what is it you wish to know about Ashley?" she finally asked, looking as though her curiosity had been satisfied at last.

The familiarity with which Molly said the woman's name indicated to Ashton that the inn's proprietress had indeed known the woman far better than she had previously indicated. Now what bothered her was why Molly should have suddenly decided to be so obliging. "Just how well did you know her?"

"We were very close. She was the daughter I never had," answered Molly without a blink. "Ashley moved in with me right when she went to work for Doc Breyer." Her words were spoken in rhythm to the rocking of her chair. "She was so proud of that nursing degree of hers. Said she had always wanted to help folks who were sick and needed a hand. Such a sweet thing," sighed Molly. "She just couldn't do enough for you." Pale gray eyes settled on Ashton's face. "She was pretty as a picture. Just like you."

Ashton reached for the lightly veined hand and gave it an affectionate squeeze. "You didn't know her before she came to Fox Run?" she asked a few minutes later.

Her silver head shook slowly. "She just showed up on the porch one day with her trunk beside her. She told me she had just finished college in Cullowhee and had gotten a job in Fox Run. I believe she said that the train conductor recommended my rooming house." A faraway look clouded Molly's face. "After I got to know her, I never could bring myself to charge her a dime for board." Molly smiled as she remembered. "She used to put up such a fuss! Finally I had to tell her a little white lie," she chuckled. "I told her my health wasn't so good anymore and that it was a relief to me to have a registered nurse in the house. Fact of the matter was that after I got to know her, I felt like she was more than just a boarder. She was just like family."

Ashton's curiosity was heightening with each passing minute. It became more and more difficult not to blurt out her questions all at once. "Where was she from originally?"

"She never told me, and I never asked. Figured it wasn't my place to ask questions. If she'd wanted me to know, she'd have told me. And she never did. I'm pretty certain that she wasn't from around these parts."

Cav stretched out his legs. "How could you tell?"

Molly's distant smile returned. "Once she complained of backaches, and I gave her an old mountain remedy of yellow root tea. Why, she thought that was the craziest thing she had ever heard tell of. Funny thing, that tea cured her back pains better than any medicine she had tried. We laughed a lot over that."

"How long did she live here with you?" asked Ashton.

"Seven years before . . ." Molly gulped.

"Before what?" urged Ashton. She sensed that she was finally making some headway.

"Before she was killed in that horrible automobile wreck." Molly shielded her eyes. A few minutes later, composed and collected, she lifted her head. "Poor babe. I never saw her any happier than she was the day she left town with—"

Ashton was sitting on the edge of the settee. "With?"

"Her gentleman friend," answered Molly quietly. She reached inside the sleeve of her robe and brought out a handkerchief.

Ashton fell back against the plump cushions. Finally, she was getting somewhere. Her suspicions that Hampton and Ashley had been intimately involved were about to be verified.

"He died with her." Molly dabbed at her eyes.

Ashton was shocked. She had been so certain there was a connection between Breyer and Ashley. "I see," she said quietly.

Pained lines deepened across the old woman's face.

For the moment, Ashton wanted to take Molly in her arms and comfort her. As much as she hated putting her through such an ordeal of remembering, she knew that she could not let up until she received the information she needed. Her life could very well depend on it. Cav's arm on her shoulder gave her the encouragement she needed to continue her questioning.

"Was Ashley forced to leave town because of a scandal?"

Molly winced. "That word has such a tawdry sound to it." Her thin arms tightened around her cat. She squeezed him close to her bosom. "Only three people ever knew for sure. Two of them were killed."

"Knew what?" urged Ashton, the suspense building inside her. She felt as if she had no business asking these questions, but she had no choice.

"About her and Doc Breyer," answered Molly.

Ashton caught her breath. "Hampton Breyer's father?"

"He was old enough to be her father," continued Molly without answering. "At first I thought it was some kind of hero worship. She fell head over heels in love with him just like he was a young Prince Charming. I saw it happening all along. When Doc's name was mentioned, her face would get all aglow and those big brown eyes of hers would light up. He was the same way," she remembered aloud. "Before she got here, he just accepted the rut his life was in. Then, all at once, he began to look like a man who had a purpose in life. He loved her. You could see it written all over his face." Molly's head shook sadly. "I tried to warn her of the consequences. She said she knew their love was all wrong, but she wouldn't want to live without him. There was never any doubt in my mind about his intentions. He wanted more than a back-street affair. Told me so himself more than once." Her chair stopped rocking. She sat erect and rigid. "Poor man! He deserved a little happiness. That wife of his had him between a rock and a hard place most of the time he was married to her. When she found out about Ashley, she played that wronged wife bit to a hilt. And then she found out Ashley was expecting—"

"There was a child involved?" blurted Ashton suddenly.

Molly nodded, then continued. "When she found out Ashley was expecting, Faye told the both of them that she'd just as soon see them rot in hell than free Hampton, Senior."

"What happened?" Ashton found herself caught up in Ashley Kiel's bittersweet love affair.

Molly's weary shoulders shrugged. "They just had to resign themselves to the fact that Faye would never give him a divorce."

Cav leaned over and stoked the fire. "So what happened after the baby came?"

"Most folks suspected Doc was the daddy, but nobody said a word about it," she answered with a heavy sigh. "They all liked him, and it was pretty much common knowledge that he had more than his share of problems with that wife of his. Mean as a snake, she was. She died a few years back. I just bet old Faye Breyer has Lucifer himself sweating!"

"And so she knew about Ashley and her husband?" queried Ashton, trying to get the old woman back on track.

Molly fidgeted in her seat. "You bet she knew. Taunted Doc about it every minute of the day, but she still refused to give him a divorce."

"How about Hamp and Judith? Did they know?" inquired Ashton and Cav simultaneously.

Molly nodded. "At the time, Hamp was away in law school, and Judith was off at one of those fancy finishing schools." Her look soured. "You can rest assured Faye made it a point to tell them everything. No doubt she poisoned their minds with a few stories of her own in the process."

"What kind of stories?" asked Ashton, curious.

Molly rolled back her eyes. "Silly stories. Stuff like Doc was going to run off with Ashley and leave his real family sitting high and dry and without a penny to their names."

"Poor Ashley," remarked Ashton. "Her life must have been miserable."

Molly nodded. "That girl put up with a lot. She loved him so fiercely. That's for sure. Swore no matter what she'd stick by him through thick and thin. And she did." Her words were filled with pride. "Not once did she ask him to run off with her and their little girl. Mind you, if she had, he'd have done it in a minute. Ashley said all along she didn't want to cause any more problems than what they had created already. So they just went on with life like before. I kept the child while Ashley went back to nursing, and Doc was over here every evening just like before. Folks sort of accepted things as they were and let them be." Her voice trailed to a whisper. "Then one day . . ." Molly stopped. Her head dropped, and her eyes refused to look any place other than her lap.

"Then one day what?" urged Ashton, sitting on the edge of her seat.

Her features tired and drawn, Molly looked from one to the other.

"Then?" prodded Ashton anxiously.

The old woman took a deep breath. She winced. Suddenly, she looked very vulnerable and very weak.

"I'm sorry, Molly," said Ashton softly. "I had no idea this would upset—"

Molly silenced her with a wave of her hand. "Then one day," she began again with words that were strong and determined, "Doc just up and decided he was tired of living a lie. He loved Ashley so. The little girl was his pride and joy, and he knew he just wasn't going to be happy until they were living together like a real family. Five years had gone by and Faye was no closer to giving him a divorce than she had been the first time he asked. Hamp and Judith were grown, and I reckon he just figured he had taken care of his obligations and it was time to do what he wanted for a change."

She absently ruffled Sebastian's fur as she continued. "Ashley objected at first. Said she didn't want to be the cause of Doc doing something he might regret later, but eventually he convinced her that his life meant nothing without her and their child. And she relented."

"And so they left Fox Run." remarked Ashton, hurrying her friend along. "Then what happened?"

"Doc had put in for a job at Duke and got it. The three of them were off to Durham," she said, her voice sad. "I didn't know whether to laugh or cry. Selfish of me, I guess, but I had come to think of Ashley as family. Anyway," she sighed, her shoulders drooping. "That's where they were going when . . ."

Ashton completed the sentence for her. "When they were killed."

Molly nodded. Her head was heavy. "That's right, dear. When they were killed in that horrible automobile accident."

Cav finally broke the silence which followed. "How long ago was that, Molly?" he asked. "For some reason, I thought Hamp's dad had been dead quite a few years."

"He has," said Ashton, her face paling. "Both he and Ashley have been dead for twenty-five years." She looked to Molly for confirmation. "Right?"

Her eyes closed, Molly nodded. "You're right, child. Twenty-five years. When did you realize it?"

"Just this very minute." Ashton sunk deep into the corner of the settee. "All this time, I've assumed that Ashley was the same age as I. How wrong I was!"

"What are you two talking about?" asked Cav, alternating puzzled looks from Ashton to Molly and back to Ashton. "Why do I get the feeling that I've missed something?"

Ashton reached for his hand and held it tightly. "I'm the one who missed something." The color was gradually seeping back into her face. "The answer was staring me in the face all the time, but I just didn't realize it."

"You're talking in circles," said Cav patiently. "What answer?"

"The first syllable in Ashley's name combined with the

last in Doc's given name," she answered. "A-S-H-T-O-N.
Ashton." She felt as though the weight of the world had
been lifted from her shoulders. "No wonder my being here
caused such a commotion. I am the daughter of Ashley
Kiel and Doctor Hampton Breyer."

Cav looked questioningly to Molly.

"That's right. She is," concurred the old woman.

Relief flooded through Ashton in one enormous wave.
The great dark door sealing off memories of her childhood
was opened at last!

Teeth clamped together, Ashton braced herself and
waited for the memories to emerge from her subconscious.
She could see it all quite plainly. White squirrels were eating bread crumbs she had left out on the well house. A
little girl with curly black braids was swinging round and
round on the merry-go-round in the park. Her mother was
singing her favorite bedtime lullaby. She could almost
hear that sweet voice. Hush little baby, don't you cry. Her
friend Doc was taking her for piggyback rides up and down
the stairs. Oh, how she loved him! He was forever hiding
presents for her in his big white pockets and sneaking her
chocolates when Molly's back was turned.

Smiling softly, Ashton turned to her old friend. No wonder she had felt such an instant fondness for the sweet old
lady. "You used to play *Old Maid* with me," she began, her
voice distant, her eyes glazed. "We'd bake gingerbread
men and have tea parties on your good silver. Once you let
me use your paints to draw my picture, and we ended up
having to repaper the downstairs corridor." She pointed to
Sebastian all cuddled in an orange and black ball on his
mistress' lap. "You had another big calico then. His name
was Buster." Her hand went to her cheek. "I was forever
dressing him up in my doll clothes. He clawed me once.
You said he was naughty and sent him to bed without supper. I saved him some of mine, though, and we were great
friends after that." She frowned suddenly. Her head shook
slowly. "Oh, no," she mumbled, her words barely above a
whisper. "I'm not sure if I can go on."

"You must, child," urged Molly. "Get it all out. If you don't, it'll haunt you the rest of your days."

Cav tightened his hold on her arm. "It's okay, babe."

Ashton nodded. She closed her eyes and took several deep breaths. Her heart was racing inside her chest. Her temples throbbed. "One day, we packed up all our belongings in a big, black trunk. Doc was taking us off on a long vacation. He promised he'd buy me a pony. I cried. I didn't want to leave you and Buster," she told Molly, smiling weakly. "But you told me you'd come visit often. Doc put down his convertible and let me sit on his lap and help drive. We sang and ate ice cream. I don't think my mother had ever been happier."

Her smile faded. She reached for her pendant and clutched the rosebud tightly in her fist. "It happened so quickly. All at once, there was another car coming right at us. No, not a car . . . a truck. Doc swerved. We skidded off the road and down a—" she gulped "—I must have been thrown out. Then there was an explosion and . . . and flames."

Ashton felt as though she were about to collapse. Every ounce of strength had been drained right out of her. She said nothing; she just sat staring off into space.

It took her a while to realize that she was shivering and that Cav's arms were tight around her.

"Are you alright, honey?" he asked.

She braved a smile. "Yes, I am. Now." Even as she answered, she knew it would take a long time to accept the revelations just disclosed to her. "Would you have let me leave town without ever telling me the truth?" she asked Molly shortly afterwards.

"I can't tell you that one way or the other." The old woman fought to hold back her tears. "I don't know the answer myself, Ashton."

Ashton stood up and walked slowly around the room taking everything in. Now, she knew why the velvet settee and lounges looked so cozy. Very little had changed in the room where she used to play. Picking up the music box, she stroked each pony with an affectionate fondness. No wonder "Rhapsody in Blue" had always been a favorite.

A few minutes later, she pulled up a stool to the rocker and sat down at Molly's feet just the way she had done countless times before as a little girl. "I know the answer. So do you," she said with certainty. "It was never a question of whether you would or wouldn't tell me. You just couldn't decide when the time would be right for you to do it."

"I had to be certain first that you were ready to know." Molly smoothed back the dark ringlets framing Ashton's face. "I suspect that deep down you've known the truth all along. That's why the name Fox Run had the power to lure you back after all these years."

Ashton nodded. What Molly had said was true. Why else would she have such a strange fascination with the town's name?

The years fell away. Once again, she was a little girl sitting with her head resting on Molly's lap.

"Why didn't you ever come after me?" she asked, her head suddenly lifting. "I kept waiting and no one ever came."

Molly guided her head back down to her knees, her fingers winding around the dark curls. "I thought you had perished with your folks," she said, her voice breaking. "Nothing was left to indicate otherwise. Had I known, I would have come after you." Her hold tightened on Ashton's shoulders. "You must believe me. I would have never abandoned my little gypsy princess."

"My little gypsy princess," echoed Ashton softly. "Yes, I remember now. You know, I used to always wonder who had nicknamed me that." Kissing the soft wrinkles of her old friend's cheek seemed natural. "I know you would have come for me, Molly, if you had only known I didn't die with my—with my parents." How odd to use that word in referring to two people other than the couple who had raised her, she mused sadly. "All these years, you've thought I was dead. How could you have known any differently?" Her thoughts returned to Monday and to the moment Molly had first laid eyes on her. "No wonder you nearly fainted when you saw me."

"You don't know the half of it, child," said Molly, excusing herself.

She scuffed back across the frayed carpeting a few moments later carrying a canvass that was nearly as large as she.

Once again, Ashton braced herself. Something told her she was about to see the face of the woman who had bore her, the woman who she thought had abandoned her at such a young age.

"This is your mother, Ashton," said Molly, turning the front of the canvas around. "This is Ashley Kiel."

Ashton's heart stopped. The gasp froze in her mouth. She could have been looking in a mirror. The resemblance was startling. Myra had been right. She really was the image of Ashley Kiel. No wonder Pop and some of the older townspeople had looked at her like they were seeing a ghost.

Cav, too, seemed noticeably shaken. "That could be a picture of you."

"Yes, I know." She reached for the rosebud. It was identical to the one her mother had around her neck. "The necklace, is it . . . ?" she choked. The words would not come.

"Yes, it's the same one," replied Molly as she propped the painting beside the rocker. "Doc gave it to Ashley the night you were born. She'd let you wear it from time to time. You used to get the biggest kick out of it." Her tone weakened. "You must have had it on when . . . You must have been wearing it that day."

Ashton could hardly take her eyes from the portrait. "You know," she said softly. "Mom always told me that my real mother had given the necklace to me so I'd always have a little part of her with me. I never could remember for sure." She lifted the rose to her mouth and kissed it ever so tenderly. "I always thought she and daddy had bought it themselves and made up that story just so I wouldn't feel rejected by my natural parents."

Nearly half an hour of quiet contemplation elapsed before she finally turned to Cav. "I think we should go now."

He nodded. "I think so, too. You both need time for all this to sink in."

Ashton managed a faint smile. She could tell he had read her thoughts and knew exactly what was on her mind. One last matter had to be resolved. There was still one more person to see. Twenty-nine years was a long time to hold a grudge!

"I suspect we both need some time alone with our memories," agreed Molly, walking them to the door. She bundled Ashton's scarf around her neck just the way she had done when Ashton was five years old. "Come back tomorrow. Won't you, dear? We've got a lot of years to catch up on."

Ashton smiled. "You're right," she sighed. "A quarter of a century, to be exact." With no hesitation, she did just just what she had been wanting to do ever since she saw the feisty old lady Monday afternoon: she gave her a big hug.

"I know this sounds silly," she said when the three of them had stepped out onto the porch, "but I've always thought of my birthday as being October first, the day the Paros adopted me. Anyway, what I was wondering is . . . by chance . . . do you . . ."

Molly needed no urging. "May first. Nineteen fifty-four. Eight-seventeen p.m." Her eyes sparkled with delight. "I was right there the minute you came into the world. After all, somebody had to assist Doc," she said with a wink.

Chapter Fifteen

ASHTON tunneled herself deeper into the mountain of patchwork stacked on top of her. She watched without her usual enthusiasm as the *Dolphins* ran back the *Colts* opening kick for an eighty-yard touchdown. Any other time, she would have liked nothing better than to curl up in bed and while away a wintry Sunday afternoon with an exciting ballgame. The setting couldn't have been more perfect; the weather outside was just made for snuggling. Inside, logs were crackling in the fireplace, and Zebo was back home dozing in his favorite spot in front of the hearth. But more importantly, the man who had given new meaning to the word love was stretched out beside her. That in itself should be enough to evict any troubling thoughts from her mind, she told herself. But it was not. The harder she tried to pay attention to the game, the more difficult it became to concentrate on what was happening on the big T.V. screen. Just yesterday, she had known very few of the details of her life before the Paros adopted her. But today, memories of a forgotten childhood were coming at her from all directions. Finally she was able to understand her aversion to automobiles. Her dislike of them had not stemmed from a fear of being abandoned again, as her folks had once rationalized, but rather from the terrifying events her young mind had associated with traveling in a car. Scenes from that horrible wreck undoubtedly flashed in her subconscious each time she rode in an automobile, whether as driver or passenger. No wonder she had always preferred to walk or bike short distances and to fly longer ones.

And those nightmares! She had always suspected there was a logical explanation for why the same scary dream tormented her sleep night after night. To be miraculously thrown clear of the accident only to witness the convertible explode into flames that engulfed her mother and Doc had been more than a five-year-old could endure. It had been only natural for her to repress her agonizing recollections of that day and the ones leading up to it rather than relive them time and time again in her mind.

Ashton nestled closer to Cav. His nearness and warmth gave her the comfort she sought. Odd, but she didn't feel any different now than she had before discovering Ashley was her mother. As far as she was concerned, she was still Ashton Paro, not Ashton Kiel or Ashton Breyer. Ashton Paro! She could never think of her natural parents as being anyone other than the two people who had raised her. She supposed a place in her heart would always belong to the man and woman responsible for bringing her into the world, but loving and accepting as parents two people whom she could hardly remember was too much to ask of herself. Ashley and Doc's tragic affair was a scene from a bittersweet movie. The illicit love they had shared had cost them their lives. How ironic! In running away together in hopes of making a life for themselves and their love child, they had unknowingly sealed their fate.

A tear escaped down her cheek. That was what saddened her the most. They had been snatched from life before their dream could materialize.

Getting used to the idea that her roots had begun in this town would take quite some time. But perhaps she had known it all along. Why else would the name Fox Run have held such a strange fascination for her the first time she had seen it in black and white on the gallium reports?

Addressing Hampton by his given name was difficult enough. Accepting the fact that she shared half her ancestry with him and his sister would take considerably longer. Obviously, he had no intention of acknowledging that. She wondered just how far he would go to insure that her biological link with the Breyers would never be revealed.

Ashton checked the clock for the third time in the past eight minutes. It was one-fifteen. At one-thirty, she'd phone his house again. Maybe by then, he'd be home. She certainly hoped so. The sooner the air was cleared between the two of them, the better. She didn't know quite how she was going to do it, but somehow she had to convince him that she had not returned to Fox Run after a quarter of a century just to publicly humiliate him before the elections. Her timing couldn't have been worse, no doubt about that. Poor Judith! No wonder she had been ready to claw her eyes out in the ladies' lounge. On the surface, it must have appeared that Ashton had deliberately showed up at the Inn on the Plaza just to spite Hampton.

Ashton reached for the telephone at the end of the first quarter, but instead she lifted her mug of hot apple cider to her lips and took a long sip. She waited another ten minutes for good measure, then picked up the receiver. What if he didn't believe her? She took another drink. That was a chance she'd have to take.

She dialed the seven digits almost automatically. Already, she had called the number at least a dozen times since leaving Molly's three hours ago.

A quick glance at Cav assured her that he would offer no objection to the decision she had made. Her options had already been shaved to one. If she wanted control of the situation, she had to take matters into her own hands.

Ashton heard Hampton's voice a moment later and swallowed hard. She had not expected him to be at home, much less to answer on the first ring.

"Mister—ah—Breyer, Ashton Paro calling. . . . I'm fine, thank you. And you?. . . . Good."

She took a deep breath. This was not the time to observe the usual social amenities. Beating around the bush would accomplish nothing. Her best maneuver would be to get straight to the point and attack the problem head-on.

"I'm of the opinion that it would be to both our advantages if we were to meet and discuss any misunderstandings that might have arisen from my visit to Fox Run."

Her voice was calm, but she made sure it was not without the strength and determination she needed to project to outsmart him. "I couldn't agree with you more. It is long overdue. . . . Yes, the sooner the better."

There was a long pause on the other end. Ashton could envision him lighting up and drawing long and hard on his first puff.

"This evening? No, I don't have any plans. . . . Nine o'clock would suit me just fine. . . . Alright, I'll see you there. Good-bye."

Frowning, she dropped the receiver back onto its cradle. "I don't like it one little bit," she told Cav. "He sounded too confident. Too sure of himself. You know, the whole time I was talking to him, I had the feeling that he had been expecting my call all along and had rehearsed exactly what he was going to say."

"Could be. I wouldn't put anything past him." Cav sat up straight. "Why so late?"

"He said he had to attend an early dinner engagement. That's not all," she continued, her face puzzled. "He suggested we meet at his office."

"Why there?"

"He didn't say, and I didn't ask him." Her lips were pursed in thought. "I wonder why he didn't want to meet at his house."

"Hard telling," he frowned. "I guess he has his reasons."

Ashton hugged her knees close to her chest. "I'm sure he does. But whatever they might be, I'm not so sure I'm going to like them."

Protective arms gathered her close. "I don't care what you say about being able to take care of yourself," he said cheerfully. "You're not going there by yourself!"

"Believe me, I'd be the last to object to that." Her cheek nuzzled his. "That's something else that has me confused. He said that there was no need to give me directions to his office because you knew where it was."

"It sounds as if he's expecting me to tag right along with you."

Ashton nodded. "I'd be willing to bet he was counting on it." She leafed through the telephone directory. "However, we are not going to play right into his hands without our own ace in the hole."

"Who're you calling?"

"Our old friend Sergeant Kelly. In case Hampton decides to lay a trap, I want to make sure we're not the ones snared in it. I'm going to ask him to stay out of view and monitor the entire conversation." She dialed the number quickly. "Sergeant Kelly, please. . . . Yes, I'll hold, thank you."

"What did he have to say?" asked Cav when she had concluded her conversation. "Or should I ask?"

Ashton couldn't help but grin. "I believe he thought that I had been smoking some of that rabbit tobacco. After all, it's not every day a complaint is registered against the pillar of the community." She burrowed back down underneath the quilts. "I just hope he's prompt and doesn't consider it his duty to warn Hampton beforehand."

"Yeah, so do I. You know, Hampton must have been awfully desperate to resort to criminal means to get his way," Cav remarked with quiet disbelief. "Who would have ever thought a man in his position would stoop so low as to terrorize you into leaving town?"

Cav's words echoed her own thoughts. Without a doubt, such desperation had been responsible for turning him into a modern-day Jekyll and Hyde. Hampton had been willing to risk his own personal and professional reputation just to wage his own senseless vendetta against her. He had proved that he had no qualms about breaking the law to insure that the skelton in his family's closet would remain where it was.

Ashton remembered something Cav's foreman had told her the day Judith and her brother had visited the construction site. Bud had implied that Doc's wife had been mentally unstable. A real looney-tune, he had called her. Perhaps some of that emotional imbalance had been passed on to her son. If that were the case, then no amount of reasoning would convince him that she had not come to Fox Run to claim her birthright or to stir up trouble for him. It still didn't make any sense! Hampton had been nearly grown when she had been born. Her birth may have caused a scandal, but surely he hadn't been emotionally scarred by it. Then again, twenty-nine years was a long time for a simmering hate to come to a full boil, she reminded herself.

Ashton tucked her head into the hollow of Cav's arm and tried to concentrate on the football game. The second half held no more interest for her than the first two quarters.

She could kick herself for not following her first impression of him. His concern over Zebo's welfare had been nothing more than a ploy to cover his own guilt and to shift her suspicion elsewhere. She should have seen through it. He was shrewd, no doubt about that. Hard telling what he had planned for tonight. One thing was certain: every move would be carefully calculated.

"You know something? I wouldn't put it past him to try to con the police into believing that we were the ones guilty of breaking the law," Ashton announced. "I'll bet he could present a very convincing argument to the court that I had come to Fox Run to blackmail him and you were my accomplice."

"You might have just hit on his tactic for tonight. That would help explain the time and the location of our meeting." Cav stroked his chin thoughtfully. "He could shift the burden of guilt onto us with no effort at all."

"Exactly!" She sat up straight. "It would be so easy for him to say that when he refused to meet our demands for money, we threatened to go to the police with accusations that we had concocted against him."

"Good thing you alerted Kelly."

"Let's just keep our fingers crossed that he shows up." Ashton winced. She didn't even want to consider what might happen if Kelly took her complaints lightly and ignored her request for assistance. Spending the rest of her life in the Transylvania County jail was not what she had in mind when she decided that her future was with Cav.

Cav chuckled.

"What's so funny?"

"You," he said.

"Me?"

Cav nodded.

"I'm glad one of us can keep a sense of humor," she said, grinning.

He ironed himself against her. "Ol' Hampton might be crafty, but you're a hell of a lot foxier."

"Think so, huh?"

He flattened her chest against his. "Something tells me he has finally met his match in you!"

Ashton rolled over on top of him. "What about you?" she couldn't resist asking.

"I was a fast learner." His fingers crept under her pullover. "I sized you up the minute I buzzed past you on 64."

He eased aside the lace cupping her breasts. Satiny mounds tumbled out to greet him. A moment later, he switched off the T.V. with a click of the remote control.

"Aren't you interested in finding out who's going to win?" she asked, winding herself tighter and tighter around him.

"I already know," he whispered.

Her lips crumbled beneath his powerful mouth. She could tell by his kiss that he was not referring to the *Dolphins* or the *Colts*.

The telephone rang a few minutes later. Ashton pried his arms and legs from around her and rolled off him, laughing. She reached for the phone, then set it down on his chest. "Well, aren't you going to answer it?" she asked after the sixth ring. "It might be important, you know."

"More important than this? You're nuts!"

She eluded his attempt enfold her. "Answer it."

He rolled back his eyes dramatically. "Hello." His expression grayed instantly. "Where?" He leaped out of bed and across to the window. "Right. I can see the smoke. . . . Alright, you contact the fire squad, and I'll round up my men and start digging ditches around it. . . . Appreciate it, Sam. I owe you one."

Ashton dashed to his side. "What's wrong?"

"That was the park ranger." He quickly pulled on his boots. "He spotted a fire up on the ridge."

"Oh, no!" She didn't have to be told what that meant. If the fire spread, the entire *Wolf Lair* project could go up in flames. "What can I do to help?" she asked, jerking her sweater back over her head.

"There's an employee directory in the top desk drawer," he said, racing down the stairs with her close on his heels. "Call Bud, Hank, the Erskine brothers, anyone else who's listed, and tell them to get up here fast. A hundred dollar bonus is in it for any man who fights the fire. Monitor channel fifteen," he shouted as he raced outside. "I'll be keeping in touch."

Ashton already had Bud on the line when the silver pickup spun out of the yard. When the last man had been notified, she stood at the window and waited. Hank's Blazer was the first to plow across the field. Bud's Bronco barrelled after it a few minutes later. She counted eighteen vehicles in all. Please let there be enough men to fight it, she prayed silently as she paced from one window to the next.

It was nearly seven before Cav raised her on the CB. "Thank God you're alright," she breathed. "How's it going?"

"Everything's under control," came Cav's voice through the receiver. "I'll be home shortly, babe. How about throwing a couple of steaks on the fire and start a bottle chilling?"

"You got a big ten-four on that one!"

The phone rang just as she was putting the finishing touches on a salad. She answered cheerfully, half expecting Cav to be calling from the office. The sound of Judith's voice on the other end quickly erased her grin.

"I understand," she assured her when Judith's monologue had finally ended. Judith's apologies for her unexcusable behavior the night before took Ashton completely by surprise. "No hard feelings? No, of course not." Her brows knitted together in silent consternation. "That's right. Nine o'clock at his office. . . . Why the change? . . . I see." She checked the time. Cav should be home in time to make it. "Perhaps it would be more convenient to meet earlier." She wanted to tell Judith that the entire matter couldn't be resolved fast enough to suit her, but she contained herself. "I agree," she said instead. "It is past time to put this whole affair to rest. . . . I'm certain I can find it. See you in forty-five minutes."

Ashton grabbed her purse and coat and waited at the door. They would have to leave as soon as Cav came home. A half hour later, there was still no sign of him. She was starting to worry. He had told her that he would be right home. The last of the steady stream of headlights had curved past the cabin a good while back.

She tried to raise him on the CB, but her call for the Silver Wolf went unanswered.

She dialed the number for the trailer and breathed a sigh of relief when the phone was picked up on the first righ. "Hello, is Cav there? . . . . Do you know where he is?" Ashton frowned. "What's he doing up at the condos? . . . . Oh, no. Was there any damage? . . . . That's a relief. . . . As a matter of fact, I do need to get in touch with him. It's pretty important. Is Bud around? . . . . Oh, Hank. You sure can. Are you sure it won't be any trouble?. . . . Great. Tell him that our appointment has been changed to eight o'clock. . . . That's right. Eight. And we'll be meeting at 506 Country Club Drive. . . . Thanks a lot, Hank. You, too."

Chapter Sixteen

Ashton jogged across the grounds of the Breyer estate toward the tower and spires that loomed a short distance away. The house was every bit as spooky as she had imagined. It could easily have been blueprinted from Hawthorne's house of seven gables.

She scanned her surroundings cautiously. Thank heaven she had a clear shot the rest of the way up to the house. The full moon was throwing all sorts of weird shadows across the woods surrounding the property. The street outside had been deserted. Even the neighborhood dogs were shirking their duty. The only sound she could hear other than her pumps shuffling the pine needles was the hammering of her heart inside her throat.

Lifting her chin from inside the fleecy collar, she dug her hand deeper into the pockets of her tweed baggies and dropped her pace to a brisk walk. There was nothing to be afraid of, she kept telling herself. Her right hand fumbled underneath the bulky brown knit for her pendant. If Hampton's intention was to harm her, he certainly wouldn't have arranged a meeting at his home, she reasoned silently.

A figure standing on the porch beckoned her closer. Ashton squinted into the darkness, her heart missing several beats. A moment later, she waved back. The relief she felt eased some of the tension mounting inside her. Surely he wouldn't try anything funny with his sister there as a witness.

Judith hurried her into the house. "Sorry you had to park on the street. I forgot to warn you," she said, taking her jacket. "I've been after Hamp all week to fix the gate buzzer, but with the elections so close, he hasn't had time to bother with incidentals like that."

"That's quite alright," returned Ashton politely. She scanned the downstairs area for the man she had come to see. He was nowhere around. "The walk was rather pleasant."

"Walk?" laughed Judith as she hung the coat in the hall closet. "It's more like a hike. That must be a good half mile from the road, and it's uphill most of the way. Let's go in the library, shall we?" She breezed on ahead. "Hamp should be down directly."

Giving one last tug to the leather braid belting her sweater, Ashton followed her through the double doors.

The air inside the library was thick with the smell of tobacco. The room was definitely Hampton's domain, decided Ashton. She did as Judith suggested and made herself comfortable in one of the thick-cushioned easy chairs. There were no traces of a feminine touch anywhere in the room. Judith, herself, looked out of place in a room where everything was either leather or mahogany.

Judith glided across to the liquor cabinet. "Care to join me in a glass of wine?"

Ashton shook her head. "No, thank you."

She settled firmly in her seat. When the confrontation with Hampton occurred, she would do well to be in complete charge of her faculties.

"I thought Cav would be joining us," Judith remarked, uncorking a bottle of wine.

"He intended to, but something came up at the last minute." Ashton felt an unmistakable tension in the air despite Judith's attempt to dismiss the meeting as a social occasion.

"Some other time, then." Judith glanced out the window.

"I don't know what has happened to Hamp. He promised me he'd be on time. I do hate to be kept waiting, don't you?"

Ashton was startled. "He isn't here?"

Judith sat down across from her. "Judge Fagen called right before we had our cocktails and asked Hamp to bring some files over to his house," she explained. "I suppose he needed to review them before court convenes in the morning."

Ashton tried to mask her frown. Now she really was confused. What happened to that dinner party he had to attend, and why had Judith given the impression that he was right upstairs?

"Is something wrong?" Judith lifted the pewter goblet to her mouth with both hands.

"No, nothing's wrong," Ashton assured her quickly. "I'd just like to resolve this entire matter as soon as possible."

"Yes, I would imagine you are anxious to do that." Judith studied her over the top of her goblet. "I certainly would be."

Ashton didn't know how to answer.

"You know, Hampton's been under tremendous pressure ever since you arrived in Fox Run," Judith said, setting her goblet down on the coffee table. "He's convinced that you've come back to ruin the Breyer good name. Not that that should excuse him, mind you," she added hastily. "I just want you to be aware of the factors motivating him."

Ashton nodded understandingly but said nothing. The accusations Judith had hurled at her last night replayed inside her head like a broken record. *You may have Hamp fooled but you can't fool me,* she had charged.

"After he saw you in Varner's," she continued, "he came home fit to be tied. He insisted that drastic measures had to be taken before you damaged us. I tried to talk him out of those dreadful things, but he wouldn't listen."

Ashton felt the hair on the back of her neck bristle under Judith's impaling glare. Hampton wasn't the only person with both opportunity and motivation!

Judith returned to the bar and refilled her goblet. "I suppose I'm as much at fault as he. I should have tried to warn you before now, but I just couldn't bring myself to betray my own brother."

"Of course you couldn't. No one would have wanted you to." Ashton made certain her casual glance at the grandfather clock in the far corner of the room went undetected. Hampton had said nothing about including Judith in their meeting. Perhaps the reason she had been omitted was the same one for scheduling the meeting at his office. Time was running out. Good God! She had been caught in the mousetrap after all!

"My brother can be a ruthless man. He'll stop at nothing to get what he wants. I learned a long time ago not to stand in his way."

Ashton unconsciously reached for her necklace the way she always did when she was nervous or confused. She only half-listened to what the woman across from her was saying. *Time is running out!* That's what the caller on the CB has warned her. The voice was so familiar. She had heard it herself before, but where? Who did it belong to? Certainly not to Hampton.

Ashton's shoulders dropped a minute later. That same voice had answered the phone at the trailer. Cav would never receive her message.

She looked up suddenly. Something Judith had just said . . . "I'm sorry. What did you say?"

Judith smiled sweetly. Her hands crossed onto her legs. "I asked if the fire had done much damage to the resort."

"Fortunately, it was spotted just in time. Cav and his men were able to contain it to the ridge." Ashton had said nothing about the fire. There was only one way Judith could have known about it. Without a doubt, she and Hank were involved together.

Ashton tried to keep her composure. She prayed Judith wouldn't detect how frightened she was. "Might I trouble you for that drink now?" she asked, anxious not to give herself away.

"Of course," Judith replied in a perfect hostess voice. "What will you have?" She breezed past, her icy fingers stabbing into Ashton's shoulders.

She cringed from the touch. "Scotch and water, please."

Ashton watched every move Judith made as she fixed the drink. What could the woman possibly hope to accomplish by stringing her along like that, she wondered. It was as though Judith were playing some kind of game with her, a game in which the stakes were life and death. Even worse, she seemed to be enjoying it!

"Here you go," she said, leaning down to deliver the drink. Eyes the color of green ice were suddenly filled with hatred. Judith's expression had changed as rapidly as a chameleon changes colors.

Ashton's skin crawled. The way Judith was staring at her neck made her certain the woman was going to go for the jugular.

Hampton's sister was quick to collect herself. Once again, she became cool and well-mannered. "By all rights, that necklace should have been given to my mother," she said matter-of-factly. "Ashley Kiel stole that just as she stole my father."

Ashton bit her lip. Now was not the time to challenge her. Judith was a time bomb set to blow at any minute.

"But no matter," continued Judith in a strange voice. "I think we'd all do well to put that whole messy affair behind us once and for all."

Ashton gathered her wits quickly. The last thing she wanted to do was to make Judith feel threatened. "I only wish your brother had that attitude," she said carefully. "All this would be so much easier then."

With her hostess gown swirling around her willowy form, Judith walked across the room and back again, her eyes never leaving her guest for one second. She had the look of a black widow poised to snare some unsuspecting prey. "Oh, he will," she said, smiling. "Between the two of us, we'll convince him." Her smile could have made an Eskimo shiver. "As I've told him already, you should not be held to account for sins committed by that slut who bore you."

Ashton gritted her teeth. "I am sorry for any unhappiness you or your family might have suffered, but blaming my mother hardly seems—"

"Being sorry isn't enough," interrupted Judith calmly. Her lips pursed thoughtfully. "It's really a shame, you know. I'm certain that under different circumstances, I would have found you most charming."

"Retribution was made twenty-five years ago," reminded Ashton softly. "You know that. My mother and Doc . . . our father . . . paid dearly for any grief and heartache they caused."

Judith's laughter was like the bray of an animal. "Our, did you say? Next thing I know you'll be lecturing me on sisterly love or something equally as ridiculous." Her eyes took on a hostile, almost vicious glare. "Don't you dare speak to me about him! He ceased being my father when he took up with that slut and let her convince him her bastard was his. My mother worshipped him. And what did he do? He left her and his children for them—for you and her!" she spat.

Ashton held her tongue. Judith could snap at any minute, and the less she did to encourage it, the better.

"He got what he had coming," Judith announced, full of hate. One hand rested casually atop the desk. "So did she, for that matter. They wanted to be together. Fine! Just fine!" She set down her glass on the polished mahogany. "Right before Mama died, she made Hamp promise to get rid of every trace of that little tramp. Everybody in town knew about him and that nurse of his. None of us could bear walking down the street. They couldn't wait to flaunt it in our faces." She removed the engraved silver lid covering the cigarette case. "Poor Mama had to suffer all alone while we were at school. She had to endure so much. How humiliating it must have been knowing that he had rewritten his will so that his whore and her bastard shared equally with us. With us!" she shrilled. "With his real family!"

Her gaze not wavering, she removed something from the case.

Ashton's heart dropped to her feet. My God! It was a pistol. One on one, she could have dealt with her, but now Judith had an undisputable edge. She watched, fear mounting, as her half-sister turned the weapon over and over in her hand.

"Hampton shouldn't have stopped with destroying your birth certificate," Judith said, the barrel pointed directly at Ashton. "Too many people knew you existed. He should have gone after you himself, but he wouldn't listen to me." She laughed softly. Even her chuckle sounded evil. "You know, he tried to make me believe you had come to Fox Run to look for some silly kind of a rock. Imagine, thinking I'm so gullible." Her smile vanished. "But he couldn't fool me. I'm not stupid. The both of you can talk until you're blue in the face, but I'll still know the real reason you came. You're not getting one red cent from me. The Breyer estate belongs to me and Hamp. I'd just as soon see you rot in hell before I'll let you take what's rightfully mine!" She waved the gun wildly in front of her. "Get up!"

Taking extra pains not to make any sudden moves, Ashton rose slowly. "I didn't come here for money or to cause any embarrassment to you and your brother." As inconspicuously as possible, she scanned the room for another way out. There was only one, and Judith was in the way of it. "I didn't even know we were . . . we were related until yesterday. I swear it." She tried to stay calm and convincing. "Please, sit down and let's talk this out," she suggested. "I'm not here to torment anyone. You must believe me." She waited for some kind of response. None came. "You said it yourself a moment ago. We shouldn't be held accountable for our parents' mistakes."

Judith's expression became demure, her voice almost apologetic. "I didn't want to kill you. Really, I didn't, but you left me with no other choice. I tried to get you to leave town, but you just wouldn't."

"I know. I understand," she reassured her, certain that

she was making some headway. If only Judith would take a few more steps to the right, the path to the door would be clear and she could make a run for it. "I really am sorry," she continued, keeping her tone even and smooth. "Had I known the truth, I would never have come to Fox Run. I wouldn't hurt you or anyone else. And I know, Judith, that deep down, you really don't want to hurt me, do you?"

Judith blocked the door with several sudden steps to the side, still brandishing the gun in Ashton's direction. "You're wrong, dear girl. Ever so wrong! I want to make you suffer just the way you made me and my mother suffer all these years. Father wanted you, and he shall have you. I shall make it my gift to him," she announced almost gaily. "Quite daughterly of me, don't you agree?"

Ashton knew there was no point in trying to convince her otherwise. Judith's sick mind was already made up. Nothing Ashton could say would make her think any differently. She lacked the mental capability to exercise reason or to understand any attempt at reasoning at that moment.

She stole a glance at the clock on the bar. It was nine o'clock. If only she had taken the time to notify Sergeant Kelly of the change of plans. If only . . . If only . . . So many if onlys were going through her head, she couldn't think straight. Swallowing hard, she took a grip on the situation and herself. Judith had every intention of killing her. Catching the crazed woman off-guard was the only chance she had of preventing it. There was only one way she could get out of that house alive, but she had to maneuver just a little closer to her captor first.

"You know, all this time, I thought Hampton had been the one responsible for masterminding all those accidents," she said smoothly, deciding to try a different approach. "It seems I gave credit to the wrong member of the family. You were ingenious. There's no denying that."

Judith looked pleased. "I've already summoned the police twice this evening to investigate strange noises out back," she announced proudly. "Here I am in this big house all alone. The housekeeper has a night off. My brother's working late at his office. If someone tried to break in, I'd be forced to shoot them in order to protect myself." Her head shook with feigned sadness. "Such a shame to mistake a visitor for a prowler. I'll be so distressed, I'll have to have a sedative for sure."

Ashton kept her distance for the moment. When cornered, wild animals attacked. She had a feeling the same basic instinct governed Judith, too.

She nodded to the table where she had left her highball glass. "You don't mind, do you?"

"Of course not," she replied sweetly. "Cheers."

Ashton moved slowly, one eye on Judith. "So that's why you had me park on the street?" she asked, wanting to keep Judith talking.

Judith looked quite pleased with herself. "Brilliant. Right?"

"Almost foolproof." She forced a swallow of liquor. "There's only one slight problem you seem to have overlooked."

The gloating smile vanished. "What—what are you talking about?"

Ashton tightened her grip on the glass. Her hunch had better pay off. She really was running out of time. "Why, Hank, of course. He's the only one who'll know that your shooting me wasn't an accident. After all, you did pay him off to carry out your plans."

"He'll keep quiet," she said with a shrug of her shoulder. "I've paid him more than enough to insure his silence."

"Maybe so. But he could make a lot more money blackmailing you. Especially if Hampton wins on Tuesday," she added.

Judith returned no quick retort. Eyes narrowed, mouth set and cold, she considered the possibility.

Ashton was certain Judith had taken the bait. She watched as the gold-bangled hand dipped lower and lower. She could feel her heart pumping harder and faster. Blood raced at top speed through her veins. Finally the pistol was pointed at the floor.

With no time to spare, Ashton threw the scotch and water into Judith's face, and in the same movement she drew back her leg and kicked the gun away just as she had been taught in self-defense class.

The pistol went skipping across the hardwood floor. Ashton scrambled over the Oriental rug to retrieve it.

"I believe I can take it from here," came a voice from behind her.

Ashton tensed, but then relief washed over her. Never did she think she could be so glad to hear Sergeant Kelly's deep Southern drawl!

Judith ran to his side. "Thank God you came. She tried to kill me."

Ashton handed him the pistol. "How long have you been here?"

His stogy rolled to the corner of his mouth. "Long enough to see that you didn't need me. That's some fancy footwork you got there."

"How did you know I'd be here?"

"It wasn't because somebody thought to call and inform me of the change of plans," he answered with gentle gruffness. "That's for sure!" He took three bullets from the chamber then stuffed the pistol under his belt. "Mr. Breyer caught me nosing around his office. Lucky for you, Cav showed up in time to set things straight. Seems ol' Hank couldn't wait to spill the beans after your young man beat the hound out of him." He took hold of Judith's arm. "Come along, m'am. You've got a lot of explaining to do."

Judith tried unsuccessfully to jerk away from his hold. "Me? You've got it all wrong, sergeant," she insisted. "I'm the victim. Not her." She pointed an accusing finger at Ashton. "She's the one who's guilty. She tried to blackmail me, and when I refused to pay her price, she swore she'd kill me," she explained with wide-eyed innocence. "I managed to get behind the desk and take my brother's gun out of the drawer. We fought. The gun slid out of my hand. She got to it before me, and turned the gun on me." Judith clung to his arm. "You believe me, don't you? You saw it yourself. She was pointing the gun at me!"

"Save it for the judge, lady," remarked the sergeant as he ushered her out. "He gets paid to listen to sob stories. I don't."

Cav rushed in past them. "Thank God, you're safe!" he exclaimed, gathering her close. "I was so afraid we'd be too late."

"Hey, bub," called out Sergeant Kelly after turning Judith over to two of his men. "I wouldn't get too close if I were you. Those legs of hers ought to be registered as deadly weapons."

"What's he talking about?" asked Cav, confused.

"I'll explain later." Tender fingers caressed his jaw. "Looks like you're the one who got all the battle scars. Poor baby."

Cav rubbed the side of his face. "Hank throws a hard punch. Lucky for me, mine are a lot meaner."

She breezed her lips across the bruises. "There. That should make it all better."

"If you think that's all I get for bravery above and beyond the call of duty, you've got another thought coming!"

Laughing, she led him over to the bar. "How did you figure out that Hank was involved?" she asked as she folded some ice cubes into his handkerchief.

Cav held the ice pack to his face. "We got the fire put out a little too fast to suit him. When the rest of the guys headed home, he tried to detain me—permanently." He winced. "Good thing I retained a few moves from my days on the gridiron."

A commotion in the foyer drew her attention from Cav's injuries a moment later. Ashton watched, still somewhat stunned by the surprising turn of events, as Judith was wrested, screaming, from her brother's side. "She told Sergeant Kelly a few minutes ago that she was the victim, not

I," she sadly recalled. "I guess in a way she really was. Her obsession with the past turned her into a crazed woman."

"If Judith is a victim, it's her own doing." Hampton Breyer entered the library, his steps sluggish and heavy. Gone was his impervious air. In its place was one of troubled concern. He looked old and tired. Every feature bore the weight of the agony gnawing away inside him. He watched, his head shaking sadly, as the patrol car sped into the darkness. "You must not hold yourself responsible for my sister's condition, Miss Paro—Ashton," he corrected in a gentler tone. "As much as I love her, I'd be the first to admit that she had—has—serious mental problems." He flipped open his gold case and took out a cigarette. "If not you, then something else would have set her off. The roots of her emotional instability go back many years. Neither you nor your mother had anything to do with it, I assure you." He took a long drag, then exhaled the smoke slowly. "Judith has been under psychiatric observation most of her adult life. She's been in and out of a private sanitarium for the past eight years." He paced back and forth across the room, one hand at his mouth, the other hanging limply by his side. "But I shan't trouble you with the details. At any rate, in September, her doctor assured me that she was fully capable of functioning in society and leading a perfectly normal life." Sighing heavily, he blew smoke high above his head. "Obviously, he was wrong."

"I don't understand," said Ashton quietly. "The first time I met her, she seemed fine."

Hampton slumped down in the big wingback chair behind his desk. "Judith lapses in and out of violent fits of depression. One minute, she's poised and relaxed. The next, the slightest provocation can send her into an uncontrollable rage. She's a lot like our mother used to be in that respect." He gave Ashton a weak smile. "So you see, she hasn't been truly fine for quite some time now. I suspect it's all just a game with her. She knows that if she behaves in a manner that's acceptable, she's rewarded. If her behavior is erratic, then she has an excuse for any action that deviate from the norm."

"What will happen to her now?" asked Ashton. Like it or not, she and Judith shared the same father. That in itself created a bond between them.

"Most likely, I'll be able to have her declared incompetent to stand trial," he answered thoughtfully. "With her past record, that shouldn't be too hard to do. Then, she'll be recommitted at Appalachian Hall." He lit another cigarette off the one he was about to extinguish. "In five years or so, she'll be declared fit, and the doctors will once again release her into my custody. It's all a vicious cycle, you know."

"I've heard the same thing said of life," remarked Ashton softly. She found herself pitying him as much as she did his sister. He looked like a defeated man. How had Molly put it about Doc? A man without a purpose.

"I thought you were the one responsible for all those things that happened to me," she told him, realizing that the two of them shared that same bond as well.

Hampton's smile was genuine. "I didn't do much to alter your opinion, did I?"

She returned his smile with one that was as sincere as his. She was seeing him in a different light. Something told her that he had let her think he was the bad guy so she wouldn't attempt a head-on confrontation with Judith. He would be the last to admit it, but he had actually tried to protect her from risking her life.

Hampton inhaled the smoke, then released it slowly. "I hadn't even intended to tell Judith you were in Fox Run, but when I came home from the office on Monday, she had already caught wind of it. Outwardly, she seemed to be nothing more than a little curious. On the inside, though, I would imagine she was boiling. Apparently, from what you told me, it took hardly any time at all for her to contact Hank and employ him to do her dirty work."

Ashton squeezed Cav's hand. "I guess I made his job even easier when I moved up to *Wolf Lair.*"

Cav shook his head. "Can you believe it? They were two suspects we eliminated right off the bat."

Several minutes of quiet deliberation passed before Hampton came out from behind his desk. "I believe this belongs to you," he told Ashton as he handed her a large envelope. "In it you will find a copy of your birth certificate. The original will be returned to the courthouse files tomorrow morning."

Ashton remembered what Judith had told her about Mrs. Breyer's dying wish. "Why didn't you destroy it?" she asked, half suspecting that she already knew the answer.

"Nothing conclusive was ever found to substantiate or disprove my mother's claim that you had been killed in that automobile accident." He snuffed out his cigarette. "Knowing that, I couldn't permit myself to do away with that one piece of evidence that even proved you existed."

Ashton unfastened the clasp of the envelope, then snapped it back into place.

"Aren't you going to open it?" asked Cav.

She shook her head. "I'm not ready for that part of my life. Not just yet." She looked at Hampton. "It's going to take some time to get used to it all."

"I understand," he said with a slight nod. "When you do open it, you'll also find a copy of my—of our—father's will inside. I believe you'll find its contents self-explanatory. We can discuss it and make the arrangements necessary to fulfill the terms. When you're ready," he added, smiling gently.

Her eyes met his. "Yes, when I'm ready," she echoed softly.

Ashton slipped her arm through Cav's. "I'd like to go now," she told him.

"Whatever you say."

She looked at her half-brother, knowing something else should be said but not knowing quite what. A part of her wanted to reach out to him. The other part held back.

Ashton decided that there would be plenty of time to mend fences later.

"Thank you. Thank you for everything," she finally said when they reached the door.

"No need to thank me." Breyer started to reach for her arm, then changed his mind. "When you decide you're ready to talk, you just let me know. I reckon we've both got a lot that needs saying."

Chapter Seventeen

C<small>AV</small> S<small>TRETCHED</small> out on the sofa with his head resting on Ashton's lap. "Good thing those steaks were ready to go on the fire. I was starved."

"Mm," she sighed.

"Is that Mm an Mm, I'm happy and content, or Mm, I'm in no mood to communicate?"

Ashton grinned. "Actually, it's a little of both. I am most definitely happy and content." Her lips smacked his. "And Mmmm, I would like to communicate, but conversation is not exactly what I had in mind."

Cav rallied himself to his feet. "I believe I know exactly what you have in mind." He offered her his arm. "Shall we retire upstairs?"

"You learn fast. I like that in a man," she laughed, hooking her arm through his.

He poured them each a glass of champagne a few minutes later. "Alright, what shall we drink to?"

She curled up on the bed next to him. Her eyes probed his. "How about to us?"

"To us." He lifted his glass to hers. "Whoops, wait a minute. Not just yet," he said, pulling back his glass.

"What's wrong?"

"Close your eyes."

"What for?" She made a funny face. "Is this another one of your games?"

Cav flashed her one of those lopsided grins that had first charmed her. "Just do as you're told, please."

She acquiesced. "You know, you're going to have to learn a thing or two about women. First of all, they do not—"

"Shhh!" His lips hushed her. "Any lesson I need to learn, you can teach me. Deal?"

Her heart beat louder and harder. "Deal." She opened her eyes. "Well?"

"Where were we? Oh, yes." His glass clicked against hers. "To us."

Her glass halted its course midway to her mouth. "What's this?" Her fingers were trembling so she could hardly fish the ring out of the glass. "It's beautiful," she whispered as she held the emerald and diamond band up to the light. "Beautiful!" She remembered having uttered the same words the first time she had seen it, in the antique shop the day before in Asheville. That was the same shop he had gone back to later by himself, claiming he had left his keys there on the counter!

"Good thing you fell for the old lost key trick." He slipped the ring onto the third finger of her left hand. "Now it truly is beautiful." He gathered her close to his chest. His words drifted through her curls. "We're a lot alike, that ring and I."

Ashton wound her arms tight around him. "How so?"

"We both need you," he said. His eyes took command of hers. "Without you, neither it nor I will ever be complete."

She could hardly believe her ears. "Oh, Cav, I love you so very much."

"Enough not to leave *Wolf Lair* on Wednesday?"

She laughed through her tears. "Enough not to leave *Wolf Lair* ever."

Ashton hugged him as though she were afraid he would vanish into thin air if she let go. There was no doubt about it. She had more at stake in Transylvania County than she had ever thought possible. Not too long ago, her past had occupied much of her thoughts, but now it was the future that mattered the most.

"Call it destiny, or fate, or coincidence—whatever you like," she said as she shaped the outline of the gold rosebud dangling between her breasts, "but some unknown force brought me to Fox Run. Of that I am certain!"

"You mean to sort out your childhood?"

She shook her head. "No, silly, to find you."

"Hey, what happened to that nightgown you were telling me about in Asheville?" he asked when he released her a short while later.

"You mean the real slinky one?"

He nodded.

"One second, please." She scooted out of bed, then returned a moment later with a wisp of black silk and satin. "You mean this old thing?" She held it up so that it would hang down in front of her.

Cav's eyes nearly popped out. "That's it!"

Ashton draped it over the bedpost. "See, I learn real fast, too."

He sandwiched her between his manly form and the patchwork quilt. "Mmmm, my kind of woman."

"Mmmmm," was all she could say.

THE VELVET GLOVE

An exciting series of romances laced with mystery and intrigue.